Jealous 2: The Bitch That Has My Man

By: Kellz Kimberly

D1530505

*Text **KKP** to **22828** for Updates, Spoilers, Giveaways, Announcements, & So Much More!!!!!*

Prologue

I turn my cheek music up and I'm puffing my chest. I'm getting ready to face you, can call me obsessed. It's not your fault that they hover I mean no disrespect. It's my right to be hellish I still get jealous. 'Cause you're too sexy, beautiful and everybody wants a taste that's why I still get jealous.

I was in the bed, trying to fall asleep, when I heard my phone going off. It was playing Nick Jonas' song "Jealous" which is the ringtone I set for Messiah. I was happy that he was calling back, but pissed off at how long it took him.

"Hello?" I said, answering the phone.

"Fuck Messiah," I heard someone moan.

"Hello?" I said again. Nobody answered, but I could hear people talking in the background.

"Amara, you don't ever have to worry, I'ma always be there for you and the baby," Messiah groaned.

"Mhmmm, you love this pussy, don't you baby?"

"Hell yea."

"Tell me you love me daddy so I can cum all over this dick," Amara hissed.

"I love you baby," I heard Messiah say and I hung up the phone.

I sat in the bed, stunned by what I just heard. This bitch was really pregnant by my fucking man and my so called man was over there telling that bitch he loved her like I didn't blow up his phone earlier. Tears started to fall down my face, but I quickly wiped them away. Messiah and Amara done fucked with the wrong one, and I was going to show them just who the fuck Julani Marie Cortez was.

I got out of bed, turned on my light and quickly found something to wear. I wanted to call Phallyn so she could ride out with me, but seeing how things went earlier, I figured this would be better if I went alone. I grabbed my .22 out my purse and my car keys, and was headed to the door. I was moving so fast that I walked right into Cree's chest at the front door.

"Julani, where are you going in a rush, and why are you dressed like you 'bout to body someone?" Cree laughed.

"I have to go handle something," I told him, locking the door.

"Then I'm going with you," Cree said, jumping in the passenger seat.

"Cree, I don't need you coming with me. I'm a big girl, I can handle this," I told him.

"I don't know what you are trying to handle, but I do know you're pregnant with a baby that could possibly be mine."

"Thanks for reminding me," I said.

I pulled my iPod out of the glove compartment and scrolled until I found Trey Songz "Smartphone". I hit the play button, hooked it up to the speakers in my car and pulled off. While Trey Songz was singing about lying to his chick's face, tears were flowing down mine. I was heartbroken, but most of all, pissed off because my father and Phallyn were right. They both told me that Messiah wasn't shit, but my dumb ass didn't want to listen, and now I had to find out the hard way.

"Julani, why you listening to this depressing ass song?" Cree asked, turning it down.

"Cree, now is not the time," I told him, keeping it short.

"Let me guess, it has something to do with that other nigga. What he do now, did he call you by accident and you heard him having sex?" Cree laughed.

I looked at him with the deadliest look that I could muster up, causing his laughter to fade.

"Julani, you can't be serious, he really did that shit? Man, I already told you that nigga wasn't bout shit."

Ignoring the little that Cree had to say, I drove right on to the grass that was outside of Amara's house. I got out with my gun in hand and started banging on the front door. Nobody was answering the door fast enough for me. I searched their yard for a big enough rock, and when I found one, I picked it up and threw it right through the window. It was around four in the morning and I was out here acting like a mad woman. I honestly didn't care because if I was heartbroken, then that bitch had to be heartbroken too.

"What the fuck?" I heard Messiah yell from the inside.

"Messiah, bring your dog ass out here, now!" I yelled.

"Julani, what are you doing here and why the fuck you throwing shit through my windows?" Messiah yelled, coming outside.

"Fuck you and these windows. You didn't see my four missed calls?"

"You out here acting up over missed calls? Man, go ahead with that bullshit," Messiah said, dismissing me.

"Nah, I came over here to tell your bitch congratulations," I smirked.

"Oh bae, you told her the good news? Or did you get my little phone call?" Amara said, coming outside and standing next to Messiah like he was some type of prized possession. The sight of those two made me fucking sick to my stomach.

"Yea, I got your little phone call, but guess what bitch, you aren't the only one that's pregnant."

"Messiah, what the fuck is she talking about?" Amara said, hitting Messiah in the arm.

"Oh, he didn't tell you, we sister wives now bitch. You ain't ever going to get rid of me!" I yelled, charging towards Amara. Messiah grabbed me and pushed me back, causing me to fall on the ground.

"My nigga, you put your hands on the wrong one," Cree said, walking towards us. This nigga was so quiet that I forgot that he was even here.

"Juju, come get your bitch boy before I lay his ass out and put him six feet under," Messiah said, getting in Cree's face.

Before I could intervene, Cree punched him in the face and the two of them started to go at it. I took a step back and just looked at all the chaos that I caused, all because I was jealous of what another woman had. I shook my head and started walking back to my car because I was truly embarrassed by the whole thing. I looked back one last time at Messiah and Cree fighting, before I got in my car and drove off.

****

It has been two days since I went over to Amara's house, acting a fool. The only person that I was talking to was my father. I had both Cree and Messiah blowing my phone up, but I refused to take either one of their calls. Phallyn had stopped by my house a couple of times to check on me, but I was keeping her at arm's length too. I had too much going on in my life right now and I just didn't want to be bothered with anyone. For the past two days, I kept replaying what happened, over and over in my head. I couldn't believe that I acted that way and it was all over a dude that really didn't want me to begin with.

"Julani, open the door!" I heard Messiah yell outside.

I got off the living room couch and looked out the window to see Messiah standing there with a bouquet of roses. I didn't want to answer the door for him, but I still had a soft spot for him. I reluctantly opened the door and allowed him to come in.

"Messiah, what do you want?" I sighed.

"Can we at least sit and talk?"

"No, we can stay right here because you won't be staying long."

"I just want to say sorry for everything that happened the other day. I never meant for you to find out about Amara that way and after you left, I told her that we were done for good."

"That's nice to know Messiah, but I honestly don't care."

"Julani, don't say that. We have a baby together, we can make this work," he said, caressing my cheek.

"This baby might not even be yours," I told him, pushing his hand away.

"What do you mean it might not be mine? Who the fuck baby could it be?" he yelled.

Messiah had this crazed look in his eye that made me a little nervous. I took a couple steps back, but he yanked me by the collar of my shirt.

"Messiah, please let me go," I begged.

"You let that nigga fuck you Julani? You're trying to tell me that the baby could be his?" Messiah said, pulling a gun out from his waist.

"Messiah, what are you doing?" I asked nervously.

"Julani, I hope you don't think that I'm just going to sit back and let you carry another nigga's seed," Messiah said with tears in his eyes.

He shoved me against the wall and pointed the gun at my stomach. I closed my eyes, scared for me and my unborn child's life. I heard the gun go off and then felt the sting as the bullet ripped through me. I fell to the floor with tears in my eyes; I couldn't believe that Messiah had just shot me. People always said that jealousy was the ugliest trait, I guess I understood why now.

Chapter 1: Julani

"OH SHI!" I jumped out of my sleep, clutching my chest as if I was trying to clutch my pearls. My hands roamed freely over my stomach, looking for the bullet wound. The dream I had of Messiah shooting me in my stomach seemed so real. I was a strong believer in dreams having a deeper meaning. That dream, or should I say nightmare, was my wake up call. It was the fact that Messiah chose to shoot me in my stomach, out of all the other places he could have aimed. Even though it was a dream, I got a closer look at the type of person Messiah was, and I no longer wanted him in my life.

I needed to change my life before me and my unborn child ended up hurt, or worse, dead. It was sad how a dream was my wakeup call when I had so many people trying to tell me what I was doing was wrong. Even though it took me a while to figure it out, I'm just glad I finally came to my senses. Since the whole fight happened, I haven't been talking to anyone besides my father. I made sure to talk to him at least once a day, just to keep him up to date on things, but other than that, I have really been staying to myself.

Both Cree and Messiah have been calling me nonstop the last two days. I wasn't answering because I didn't have anything to say to either one of them. At least at that moment, I didn't have anything to say to them. At this moment, however, I had a whole lot to say to both of them. If I was going to change my ways, then I would have to talk to both of them and let them know how I planned on handling things from here on out. With the way I was feeling, I didn't want to be with either one of them. Right now was the time for me to focus on me. My child would be here in about eight months. That was more than enough time to make sure I was in the right mind frame to care for my child.

I looked at the clock that was on my nightstand; it was twelve in the afternoon, which meant it was time for me to start my day. That dream was a sign for me and I planned on really taking it seriously. When everything is put in perspective for you, you can't deny the ugly things you have done. My jealousy caused a lot of unnecessary drama that should have never taken place to begin with. Messiah had a girl and I should have backed off, letting my crush go. Then I dragged Cree into this mess when all he was trying to do was be the man in my life. I was ready to start righting my wrongs because I would be damn if I brought a child into this mess I created. I wanted to play little kid games and ended up getting myself into grown woman situations. My child I was carrying in my stomach was a blessing, I just wasn't proud of the way he or she came about. I looked down at my stomach, making a promise to myself and my child.

"By the time you enter the world, I promise that I will be someone you can be proud of. I promise I will be someone that I can be proud of," I said it out loud so it would be in the universe.

I rolled out of bed and walked towards the kitchen for a glass of water. For a split second, I thought about cooking breakfast, but decided against it because I began to feel nauseous. I gulped down my glass of water, then went to get in the shower. My shower didn't last longer than twenty minutes because I had about three people to see and didn't want to be out all day. Getting out, I dried off, then quickly put lotion on my body. Moving over to my walk in closet, I stood there for a second, trying to figure out what I wanted to wear. It was the middle of July, which meant it was hot and blazing out. I honestly hated the summer because it was too hot to try and look cute. I would rather come outside naked than to wear clothes. I grabbed a cute pink maxi dress and my Chanel sandals. After getting dressed, I finger combed my curly mane, ran to the kitchen to get an apple and then was out the door. My first stop was to see the one and only Messiah. I made sure my .22 was in my bag because after that dream, I wasn't going to take any chances with his ass. I wasn't sure how the conversation was going to go, but if it did take a left turn, my .22 would help it go right. I decided to go see him first because the conversation we were going to share would be the hardest for me.

* * * *

As I knocked on Messiah's door, I felt nervous, but at the same time confident. I was nervous because I didn't know what to expect, but I was confident because I was ready for anything. I was hoping Amara was here too because I had a couple of things I wanted to say to her as well. I knocked again and it seemed like it took an eternity for someone to answer the door. When the door finally did open the man that had me out here looking a fool stood there with a smirk on his face. He had the nerve to be standing there in nothing but a pair of basketball shorts. My arms roamed his body and I couldn't help but to feel moist in between my legs. I was changing, but change was going to take more than a couple of hours.

"Baby, who's at the door? You're letting the cold air out," I heard Amara say.

"Julani," Was all Messiah said, still looking at me. We held each other's gaze, refusing to look away. The connection we had was a deep one, but it was also toxic.

I was tired of the staring contest, so I decided to end it. "Can I come in? I just want to talk," I told him.

He stepped to the side, allowing me to walk in. I let out the breath that I didn't realize I was holding. Amara stood there, staring at me like she wanted to pounce on me.

"Look, I didn't come here for drama, I just have some things I need to get off my chest," I told her.

I walked right past her ass and sat in the living room, waiting for them to join me. Even though I came here being friendly, if Amara even thought about stepping out of line, I would switch up real quick. I promise I was trying to change myself, but disrespect was something I wasn't going to tolerate.

I watched as Amara and Messiah sat on the couch across of me. Amara rested her hands on her belly, with a smirk on her face. I rolled my eyes because she really thought she was doing something. Her being pregnant did nothing for me right now, nor was I sweating it.

"Resting your hands on your stomach to emphasize you're pregnant doesn't do anything to me anymore Amara. I no longer care that you are pregnant. Matter of fact, I wish you nothing but the best in your pregnancy," I smiled, then continued. "I came here because I realized my behavior during the past three months has caused a lot of unnecessary drama. Now, I wasn't in it alone, but I am willing to take the blame for it. All I want is peace and tranquility in my life right now. As the both of you know, I'm pregnant." I had to pause for a second because this next part was going to be hard to get out.

"Juju, you don't have to worry about anything. I'm willing and ready to be there for you and the baby," Messiah spoke up.

"What do you mean you're ready to be there for her?" Amara questioned real quick. "I don't mind you being there for your child, if it's even yours to begin with. What I'm not going to do is stand around and allow you to be there for her too. Julani is grown and can take care of herself, without your help.

"Amara, you don't have a say in this shit. I created that child with her, not you. The child we have together is in your stomach, so you need to worry about that. I already told you what me and you had is done. I'm just staying here to make sure everything is straight with you and the baby. Our relationship is over, so you won't be standing around allowing me to do shit because you won't be around. The sooner you understand that we are done, the better everything will be.

Well that was definitely something I didn't expect to hear Messiah say. Ninety percent of me was happy that Messiah was leaving Amara. However, the other ten percent couldn't care less. That ten percent of me was my brain. I had followed my heart and that's how I ended up in this situation. I was now going to follow my brain.

"We are not about to have this conversation in front of this bitch," Amara spat, looking directly at me.

I laughed a little before I began to talk. I really wanted to keep my composure, but Amara was taking "Amara, there is no need for all this name calling and stuff. I came here so I could apologize and let you know there will be no more issues with me. I'm trying to be the bigger person and let everything go, but if you keep coming with the insults, I will beat that ass. Now like I was saying before the two of you started going back and forth, I'm pregnant, and it may not be yours," I told Messiah, looking him directly in the eyes.

As soon as the words I said to him registered, hurt and pain was the only thing that you could see in his eyes. I didn't have intentions of hurting him, but at the same time, I needed for him to know. I have done some fucked up things, but keeping this secret from him wouldn't be the ultimate fuck up. I clutched my purse, just in case he pulled a gun at me.

"Get the fuck out!" he barked. He had so much bass in his voice that for a minute, I thought it was my father yelling at me. I have never seen Messiah this pissed off before. I got up and started walking towards the door. I stopped in mid stride because I wanted to say something. I looked back and Messiah had his face buried in his hands, while Amara rubbed his back. I figured it would be best if I just turned around and left.

I was grateful that it went a lot better than how it did in my dream, because I wasn't ready to die just yet. It was crazy because I felt the pain that Messiah was going through. His pain hit me right in my heart, but there wasn't nothing that I could do about it. I wanted nothing more than to fix everything that I had broken, but it seemed as if I was just making stuff worse.

I got in my car and took a deep breath before pulling away. I got through the talk with Messiah, and now it was time to talk to Cree. Cree was a good dude that I could see myself falling for. He just so happened to come at the wrong time. I needed to talk to him too because he wanted a relationship, and I wasn't ready for that. I did have feelings for Cree, but the feelings I had for Messiah were stronger. It was sad, but it was the truth. As bad as I wanted my feelings for Messiah to go away, they just weren't going to disappear that easily.

I have seen firsthand how my careless actions were hurting people around me. I just couldn't bring myself to be with Cree, knowing I still had feelings for Messiah. I already put him through a whole bunch of shit and I wasn't going to continue to do it. I definitely couldn't be with Cree, while not knowing whose baby I'm carrying. That alone had me feeling like a ho. I could only imagine how I would feel if I fucked Cree and the baby was Messiah's. My whole young adult life I have prided myself on not being like these other fast ass girls in the street. I even laughed at a couple of the girls on Maury when they were trying to figure out who their baby daddy was. The joke was now on me because I was in the same boat as them. Pregnant, and not knowing who fathered my baby.

Chapter 2: Messiah

The bullshit Juju just told me hurt a nigga to the core. I know y'all probably think I'm some bitch ass nigga for the way I handled things with Julani, but y'all don't even know the half. Amara has been there for me through the good and the bad, the pretty and the ugly. Y'all find a person like that and tell me if it would be easy to walk away from them. The love I once shared for Amara wasn't there anymore, but I didn't want her riding for another nigga either. I wanted my cake and wanted to eat it; shit, I just figured that's what you're supposed to do. Shit backfired in my face though. The chick I didn't want to be with was pregnant with my baby, and the chick I wanted to be with was pregnant, but the baby might not be mine.

Damn, just thinking about the shit was killing me even more. I never pictured Julani to be the type to sleep with two men at once, but I guess you never really know who anyone is. I kicked Julani out because I couldn't stand to look at her. I had mad respect for her pops, so I would never put my hands on her, but after she told me that shit, I was tempted as hell to yoke her up a bit. I needed for her to explain to me why she did what she did. Yeah, I fucked up, but everyone fucks up, we all human. I may have swayed a little, but I planned on getting back right as soon as I found out she was pregnant. Her being pregnant put everything in perspective for me. I wouldn't have fucked Amara that night if I would have got the calls about her being pregnant. I needed to fix this shit, and quick. I'll be damn if that other nigga gets the love of my life.

"Amara, move with all that shit, ight!" I pushed her away from me and got up, heading upstairs. Amara didn't have anywhere else to live, so I was allowing her to stay here. How could I kick the mother of my child out? This was my house, so I damn sure wasn't leaving. While she slept in the master bedroom, I took one of the guest rooms.

"Just because you're mad at that little bitch, doesn't mean you can take your anger out on me," she snapped.

"Watch your mouth," I warned. I wasn't going to let her call Julani out of her name.

"Oh shit, look at Messiah coming to the little hoes rescue. You don't want me to call her a bitch, but that's exactly what she is. The baby she's carrying might not even be yours, but you are still defending the bitch. I can't believe this shit. What has she done for you that I haven't? What makes her so much better than me, Messiah? Messiah, just tell me what I'm not doing that her ass is?" I looked at her and could see the hurt on her face.

"Amara, move around with that shit. Stop asking questions you don't want the answer to." I hated when women did this shit. Whenever it came to another woman, they wanted to start asking questions and showing their insecurities.

"I'm a grown woman, trust me, I can handle whatever answers you have. You have that little bitch sitting on a pedestal, while you treat me like a peasant. I think an explanation is something that I deserve."

I sighed and looked at her, trying to figure out if this is really what she wanted. I didn't see anything that told me otherwise, so I told her ass the truth with no holds barred.

"Julani and I connect on a level that's unexplainable. It's just something about her that draws me to her. She has this take charge, boss attitude, and the shit makes my dick hard. It has nothing to do with looks because both of you are beautiful to me. The connection we have is more so a best friend type of thing. We started out as friends, then it turned into a sexual thing between us. Somehow, we ended up in a relationship. The love we shared was misconstrued."

"Misconstrued how?"

"Whenever I said I love you, it was me saying I had love for you, like on a best friend level. I knew that you were in love with me, but I couldn't bring myself to break your heart."

"Oh, you mean like you're doing now? Fuck you Messiah because everything you're telling me right now is stuff you could have said before. Instead of you opening your mouth, you strung me along like a fucking coward. I pray that I don't have a fucking son because I'll be damn if my son ends up anything like you. You are a poor excuse for a man, Messiah. Matter of fact, you're not even a man, you are nothing more than a boy. Julani deserves you since she isn't a woman either. Y'all can keep that weak ass connection y'all got because karma is a fucking bitch," she spat before storming away.

Everything Amara said was said because she wanted to hurt me. The shit didn't faze me because I had more important issues going on in my life. I refused to watch Julani be happy with anyone else that wasn't me. I was going to be the only nigga to put a smile on her face. Regardless of if the child she was carrying was mine or not, I was going to love it like it was mine. I didn't see a future for myself that didn't include Julani, so it was either her or nothing for me. Of course, I was going to take care of my child I had with Amara. Shit, I had plans on getting full custody. I wanted both of my kids to grow up in one household together. There was no way Amara and Julani were going to live together, so I needed to make a choice, and that choice was Julani.

I picked up my cell phone off the coffee table and tried calling Julani. Her shit went straight to voicemail. Her voicemail picking up didn't stop me from calling. I blew her phone the fuck up. I needed her to answer some questions for me, the same way I answered them for Amara. I was man enough to say I was insecure. I needed to know if Cree was a better man than I was. I needed to know what drove her into Cree's bed, instead of mine. Most importantly, I needed to know that Julani and I still had a future.

Chapter 3: Cree

I haven't talked to Julani since the whole shit went down a couple of days ago. I been blowing her phone, when everything popped off. After a while, I fell back. I couldn't even lie, a nigga was feeling like a straight bitch. Julani had me out here fighting niggas over her ass and she wasn't even my chick. My whole behavior was foreign; it was new to me. The way I've been acting was new to me, and I wasn't feeling the shit.

When I first met Julani, everything about her intrigued me. What attracted me to her was her confidence and her no bullshit attitude. She had an aura of a boss, but a childlike innocence. All Julani had to do was act right and she would have been a winner. She was everything I wanted in a female, but her running behind that fuck nigga, as if she didn't know her worth was a turn off. It was crazy because females always went after the dudes they couldn't have, and those same niggas were the ones to break their hearts.

A dude like me could have any chick he wanted, but I only had eyes for Julani. I wasn't being cocky or anything, I was just speaking the truth. Julani thought I was into selling drugs, when that wasn't even my hustle. Jacori was the one running shit up in Harlem. I was more so behind the scenes; I made sure all of Jacori's money came from a legit source. Jacori was my nigga from way back, so of course I had to make sure that he was straight. No one would ever be able to question how he was making his money because I made sure he was covered.

I didn't have any business to handle today, so I was chilling at the crib for the day. I was watching reruns of *The Fresh Prince,* when there was a slight knock at my door. I got up, headed over to the door, opening it without asking who it was.

"The fuck you doing here?" I asked her. Julani must have been shocked at the way I talked to her, because she stepped back a little and her eyeballs were wide as hell.

"I don't know why you're sitting there looking shocked. What you thought you were going to get a friendly greeting or some shit?"

"I didn't expect a friendly greeting, but I didn't expect such an aggressive one either."

"Yeah ight, but what you doing here Julani?" I took in her appearance and she looked good. The pink dress clung to her body, the way I wanted her to cling to mine.

"I just want to talk to you," she whispered.

"Ight," I moved to the side, allowing her to walk in.

I watched her ass jiggle when she walked past me. I closed the door, then brought her into the kitchen. Julani was the easiest woman to read. Her demeanor screamed that she was nervous. I didn't know what she was nervous for, it wasn't like I was going to kill her ass. She sat on a stool that was placed in front of my island. As soon as her ass sat down, her stomach growled.

"You hungry?" I asked. When I talked to her this time, my voice was softer and laced with concerned. If she was hungry, that meant my child was hungry too.

"No, I'm fine. I ate an apple before coming over here."

"Julani, don't play with me. I heard your stomach growl, which means my child is hungry. Get to talking and I'll make you a turkey wrap."

I busied myself making her sandwich, waiting for her to talk. I would look at her from the corner of my eye, and it seemed as though she wanted to talk, but nothing was coming out.

"Julani, I don't have all day. Say what you need to say," I demanded.

"I came over here to say that I won't be messing with Messiah."

Sitting her sandwich in front of her, I laughed a little, before taking a seat across from her. I guess she thought I was supposed to feel good about what she said, but I could honestly care less. She finally did what she should have done a minute ago. If she was looking for a fucking cookie, she wasn't going to get it from me.

"Say something to me, instead of just looking at me," she blushed. "You're making me feel uncomfortable." She bit into her sandwich and closed her eyes for a second.

"Why this sandwich taste like everything right now. It might be a simple sandwich, but it's hitting all the right spots right now. Now say something."

"Julani, what the hell do you want me to say? You stopped fucking with a nigga that wasn't right for you. The nigga isn't even for you. You should have been left him alone. Am I supposed to be happy that you finally came to your senses?"

"No, but I thought it would be something that you wanted to hear," she shrugged. If her ass wasn't pregnant, I would've slapped that fucking sandwich out her hand for the stupid shit she just said.

"Ma, you lucky you're pregnant, 'cause that sandwich would've been on the floor after that dumb shit you said. The only thing I want to hear come out your mouth is that the baby you are carrying is mine. Other than that, all I want to hear is that you're ready to take things more serious between the two of us."

"You know I won't know if the baby is yours until I have the baby. As far as us being together, that's something I'm not ready for yet."

"Hold up, Julani, so what you saying?"

"I don't want to be in a relationship right now."

"Let me get this straight. You wanted to fuck with me while you were fucking with Messiah. Now that you're not dealing with him, you don't want to deal with me either. How the fuck does that sound, Julani? You had me sitting over here, blowing your phone up for the last two days, only for you not to answer. You been treating me like I'm some bitch made nigga. I have been going toe to toe and round for round with that nigga and you weren't even my bitch. I showed you time and time again that I'm the dude you need in your life, yet you run every time you let me get close. Ever since I meant your dumbass, I have been doing things that are out of the ordinary for me." I was on ten and had to distance myself from Julani.

"Cree, you are not the only one that has been doing things out of the ordinary. The way I have been acting these last three months, isn't who I really am. I don't know who that person was, but I don't want to be her anymore. I'm not even saying I can't be with you because I'm not with Messiah. I can't be with you because I need to find myself again. I'm trying to grow up and mature all that I can before I have this baby. I need to put all my focus into me and the baby, without any distractions."

"I can respect all of that, and I understand that you want to work on a better you. All I'm saying is don't forget about a nigga. I'm trying to be with you, Julani, and show you the finer things in life."

"You came into my life at a weird time. I was too busy chasing Messiah to realize anything else. I'm sure if I wasn't running behind Messiah, you and I would probably be together. However, I can't dwell on the coulda, shoulda, woulda right now. I have to do what's best for me right now. I feel me being single right now is for the best.

"I can respect that, but at least let me be there for you and the baby during your pregnancy. I can't say that I will be on my best behavior because you got a nigga's head all the way fucked up 'bout your little ass. I will try my best to keep everything platonic. I just want to make sure you're straight, because I'm sure that fuck nigga not going to be around."

"What makes you think that?" she asked with a raised eyebrow.

"Juju, Messiah is a street nigga, not a boss. He may not be hustling on corners, but he still punches a clock," I smirked.

"Don't you do the same thing that he does?" The way she said it, one would've thought she just made a point, but she didn't.

"I'm not a street dude. Jacori is the one that is running shit in Harlem. I'm more so behind the scenes. I make sure that all of Jacori's money comes from a legit source. I guess you can say I'm an accountant."

"So you clean up his money?"

"If that's what you want to call it. I'm a boss, so I set my own hours and days I work. I can be that nigga you need Julani, you just have to allow me to be that for you. I know you said you're focusing on growth and maturity, but just keep in mind you have a nigga willing and ready to be everything you need and more."

"It may not sound like it, but I appreciate everything you're saying right now. I just need time to figure everything out. I may not be able to give you a relationship right now, but I'm willing to give you a friendship. That's all I really have for you. I'm trying to become the woman you can see yourself marrying, and for me to do that, I need to fix some things that aren't right within."

"Oh, so you trying to be the woman I wanna marry?" I said, catching on to what she said.

"No, but you know what I'm saying. I'm trying to be the woman any dude would want to marry," she clarified that real quick. She was blushing and trying to hide the smile she wore, but I caught it.

"Yeah ight, Julani. I hear everything you're saying Juju. Friends is what you want, so friends is what you're going to get. I'm here for you ma for whatever you need."

I walked over to where she was and pulled her into my chest. I felt her body melt into mine, causing me not to want to let go. Right here with me is where she needed to be, all she had to do was allow herself to give in to me.

"All you have to do is put your life in my hands ma," I whispered in her ear. My lips lightly brushed against her earlobe.

"Okay, let me get out of here," she pulled away from me and I let her.

"Where you going so quick, we could at least chill or something. I'm not going to bite, unless you want me to," I winked.

"I already told you we are friends only, so stop it. Unfortunately, I can't stay, but I'll call you later on in the week. Thank you for the sandwich."

I grabbed her hand, walking her to the front door. She gave me a light kiss on the cheek, then walked out. I watched her get in her car and pull off. I couldn't help but feel like she was taking my heart with her every time she left. I was who Julani needed right now. She wanted to do things on her own, and I was going to let her. My whipped ass would be here waiting for her when she realized that with me is where she was meant to be.

Chapter 4: Julani

After clearing the air between Messiah and Cree yesterday, I felt like a brand new person. I felt as though this was my second chance to prove to everyone that I wasn't just a spoiled brat. I had plans to change my life around, and that was exactly what I planned to do. Instead of going to Phallyn's house yesterday, I decided to have her meet me at Allure. Since we were in business together, whatever ill feelings we had for each other would have to get put on the back burner because business always came first. But business wasn't the only reason I wanted to talk to Phallyn. I honestly missed my friend. Phallyn and I damn near did everything together, so to not have her around these couple of days has been bothering me. I finally came to terms with this pregnancy and I was happy about it. I wanted her to share my joy and happiness, all the while, taking this journey with me.

Somebody real is hard to find, somebody worth all your time. Somebody who can tell you the truth, someone who loves you for you. Someone who knows all of your flaws and doesn't impose, try to control them. Let's you be free, doesn't deceive. They give you a chance to believe, believe in something. Is that too much? 'Cause I've been on the search and I'm losing my hope. Is that too much? Is that too much? Trying to find love in a world so cold. Is that too much? I just want an answer. I can't be the only one. You ain't got to be perfect, just give me a purpose to love.

Tink's song "Treat Me Like Somebody" blared through my phone. I looked at the caller ID and rolled my eyes. Since Messiah

kicked me out his house yesterday, he has been
up. I didn't answer any of his calls because I
time to cool down. However, today he has decic
on the hour. I sighed before answering my ph
tongue lashing I was about to receive.

"Hello?" I answered the phone. I heard heavy breathing, but no one was talking. I pulled the phone away from my ear to make sure that it was indeed Messiah's name on the caller ID.

"Messiah, are you there?" I questioned.

"You were dead ass serious about that shit you were talking yesterday?" he asked in a low tone.

"Messiah, are you okay?" I was truly concerned because Messiah didn't sound like himself.

"Don't try to dodge the question Julani!" he yelled. He wasn't in front of me, but I still jumped a little from the bass in his voice.

"I'm not trying to dodge the question; I just want to make sure that you are okay. I'm concerned about you."

"I appreciate that you're concerned 'bout a nigga, but I need to know were you telling the truth about the shit you said yesterday." His voice was no longer hostile.

"Yeah, it's the truth. Messiah, we were both doing things that we shouldn't have been doing. If I could change the way I acted, I would, but I can't Messiah. All I can do is accept my mistakes and ard. Just know I never meant to hurt you or to cause you

h."

"Julani, I need you to meet me somewhere. This conversation isn't meant to be had over the phone."

"I'm not sure I want to meet up with you Messiah. Plus, I have stuff I have to handle at the club." After having that dream, I wasn't sure what Messiah was capable of.

"Why you not sure about meeting up with me? Do you think I'm going to hurt you or something?"

"I don't know Messiah."

"Julani, you know me better than that. I would never intentionally hurt you," he pleaded.

"So how did you think I would feel finding out you were still sleeping with Amara? I'm sure you knew that shit was going to hurt me."

"That's different Juju, and I'm not trying to talk about that right now. It's in the past and we can't change it. Just meet me so we can talk about this. You can even pick the spot. I just need to talk to you ma." I sighed because I knew I was about to give in to his request. Messiah still held a piece of my heart. As much as I wanted to stand firm about not meeting him, I just couldn't. While he talked, I could feel his pain. I felt the pain behind each word he spoke and it killed me. I cared for Messiah and never wanted to see him hurt. If meeting with him could erase some of that pain, then I would do what was needed.

"Messiah, I will meet you, but I don't want any drama, so don't bring Amara please."

"Amara isn't coming. It will just be me and you, I promise. Just tell me where you want to meet."

"We can meet downtown Brooklyn by the IHOP."

"Do you want to go in and eat?"

"No Messiah, all we are going to do is talk, then we are going our separate ways. Meet me there in like two hours, okay?" I told him, hanging up. I didn't want to give him a chance to say anything else because I couldn't take it anymore. Here I was doing something to please Messiah, all so I wouldn't have to see him hurt.

I sat my phone down, trying to hold back the tears that were welling up in my eyes. I felt like shit and didn't know if I was going to make it through this pregnancy. Cree was fine with just being my friend, or at least he pretended to be. Then I had to have this conversation with Messiah, and who knew what was going to happen.

"Julani, are you okay?" Phallyn asked, rushing further into my office, handing me a tissue.

"Yeah, I'm okay," I told her. I wiped my eyes and blew my nose. I wanted to tell Phallyn about Messiah, but I was sure she was over my shit.

"Stop lying to me and tell me what's wrong."

"It's just Messiah. I didn't call you here to talk about that, so don't even worry about it."

"Julani Marie Cortez, if you don't tell me what the hell is the problem, I will slap you. I don't care what we are going through, if you ever need me, you know I'm here for you. Yes, I'm tired of hearing you complain about the whole Messiah situation, but that doesn't mean I won't be here to listen. I'm your best friend through thick and thin. Through the smart and the dumb times you have," she laughed.

"That was the reason I called you here. I wanted to apologize for the way I treated you. There was no reason for me to blow up at you the way I did. You weren't doing anything but being a good friend, and I realize that now."

"I may show you tough love, but I promise it's for your benefit. At the same time, I have to apologize because I should have been more supportive to you. I shouldn't have blown up when you told me you were pregnant. At that time, you needed me the most, and all I did was push you away."

"It's in the past, so let's leave it there. You're here now and that's all that really matters now."

"I'm glad we got that cleared away because I missed your spoiled ass. Now tell me what the hell Messiah said that made you cry, so I can go cut his ass."

"Yesterday morning, I woke up from a dream, well really a nightmare, that put a lot of things into perspective for me."

"What was the dream?"

"It was of Messiah shooting me in my stomach. The whole thing seemed so real and the shit was intense. Any who, when I woke up, I realized that I couldn't keep living my life the way I have been living it. I needed to change some things around that would benefit me and my child. I went over to Messiah's house, apologizing to both him and Amara. I then told Messiah the child might not be his, and the nigga threw me out, can you believe that shit?"

"Damn, I know he was hurt, and that bitch Amara was probably happy as hell," Phallyn said, shaking her head.

"You know she was, but I'm not even worrying about her. So after I left his house, he starts blowing up my phone. I figured not answering would be the best thing to do because he was pissed off. He calls me like ten minutes before you walked in, asking if he could meet up with me. I thought he was calling to curse me out, but it sounded as if he wanted to cry. I told him I would meet up with him because I didn't know what else to do. My heart ached for him because I felt his pain. I feel like shit because I caused so many people pain, and I feel like all my wrong doings are going to come and bite me in the ass."

"You can't beat yourself up because you admitted to your wrong doings and now you're trying to correct them. All you can do is move forward and be a better you. Messiah is hurt now, but he will be alright in the long haul. Have you talked to Cree?"

"Yeah, I talked to him yesterday too. I guess he thought now that Messiah and I weren't together, I was going to jump into his arms and be a couple."

"You're not?"

"Hell no. I can't be with him when I'm not even okay with being who I am. For the rest of this pregnancy, I just want to focus on me. For me, the ultimate goal is to bring a beautiful healthy baby into this world, and at the same time, be a much better me. Dating is the furthest thing on my mind right now."

"Wow!" she looked shocked. "I'm proud of you, Julani. You are really starting to sound like you are growing up."

"I'm trying," I smiled.

"Well you already know I'm going to be with you every step of the way. Do you think the guys will be there for you during the pregnancy?"

"I don't know honestly. I can tell that Cree will be sticking around, but Messiah is up in the air. Just from the phone call, he doesn't even seem stable."

As weird as it sounded, I would like for both of the men to be here for the pregnancy. I would hate for one of them not to be there, and then the child ends up being there. With both of them there, they would each get to experience the pregnancy with me. I knew it was wishful thinking because both of them in a doctor's office with me wasn't going to happen. If it did happen, I could tell you right now it wasn't going to be a peaceful visit.

"Even if they aren't there, I'll step in and be the baby's father," Phallyn giggled.

"I bet you would. But what has been going on with you? These last few days have felt like weeks since we've talked."

"Everything with me is fine, nothing has really changed. Jacori is cool and things are going good with us."

"I'm happy for you boo," I told her, and it was the truth. Jacori brought the best out of Phallyn. They honestly complemented each other.

"Thank you. But since you have been missing in action from our club, I wanted to run a couple of things by you."

"Okay, go." I felt bad about not putting in the work I should have at the club. Allure was my legacy, and I was going to make the best of it.

"Well the next four months are booked solid, but I was thinking after those four months, we should renovate. I know you did the VIP sections, but I feel like we could do even more. We have more than enough space to change this place and make it bigger than it already is."

"I was thinking about adding a restaurant to one of the floors. That should bring in more money."

"That would be a good idea," Phallyn smiled.

We continued talking about our plans for the club, and I couldn't have been happier. The plans that we came up with would definitely put us on the Forbes List within the next couple of years. The only good thing that happened to me was getting my friend back. I miss Phallyn something crazy, and I really needed her right now.

After going over the plans with Phallyn, we parted ways, making plans to go out for lunch or something the next day. It was now time to meet up with Messiah, and I was nervous as hell. I prayed everything went well with Messiah because I wasn't ready to die just yet.

Chapter 5: Messiah

I sat outside of IHOP, waiting for Julani to pull up. When I called earlier, I didn't expect her to answer. I already planned on popping up at her house because we needed to have this talk. I needed for Julani to realize that I was ready to be the man her and my child needed. I was willing to work on me, as long as she wanted to be by my side.

Amara and I were still at odds, but that was okay for me. I made sure that she ate and went to her appointments, but other than that, we had no communication. She was in her feelings about me wanting Julani, and that was exactly where I was going to leave her. I didn't have time to pacify her. I still cared about her, but the love wasn't there. I hoped one day we could get past this and she would be my best friend again, but that was probably wishful thinking.

I got a text from Julani, saying she just pulled up. I saw her park across the street and jogged to her car.

"You look good, Juju," I complimented her. The pregnancy was doing her good. She looked thicker than the last time I saw her, but that could just be my eyes playing tricks on me.

"Thanks. Messiah, what do you want to talk about because I have somewhere I need to be."

"Where do you need to be? What, you meeting up with that other nigga? Is that the reason why you wanted to meet here?" I fired off, asking question after question. Jealousy was not a pretty thing, but a nigga wasn't trying to be pretty. I wanted answers.

"No, I'm not meeting anyone Messiah. Everything isn't always about another dude. I just want to get my food and go home to eat."

"My bad, Juju. I just don't want you or my child around that nigga."

"Messiah, you have no say so in who I'm around, especially when it comes to Cree. He could be the father, just like you could. If he wants to be around me to get closer with the baby, who am I to stop him."

"I don't want to hear that shit, Julani. That baby is my baby at the end of the day, and I don't want that nigga around you or my child." I felt my blood begin to boil, but I was trying to stay calm.

"I'm not having this conversation right now. I said what it's going to be on this situation, so the conversation is over. Just tell me what you want to talk to me about Messiah, please."

"All I want to know is how could you do this to me Juju? I never expected you to go out and start creeping with the next nigga."

"I didn't mean for it to happen, things kind of just fell into place. You kept playing me to the left for Amara, and Cree was there to pick me up every time you knocked me down."

"That shit with Amara wasn't nothing. I just didn't know how to let her go and be with you wholeheartedly. You hurt a nigga to the core with that shit you told me. I just needed some time and I would've gotten right."

"You just needed time!" she yelled. "Messiah, I waited for you for a whole three months. I was fucking you for a whole three months, all the while you were fucking with Amara. If three months wasn't enough time, then I don't know what is. You want to talk about hurt. How do you think I felt to finally get a call back from you, and when I answer, it's you fucking that bitch? Not to mention, you got her fucking pregnant."

"So because I fucked up, you thought it was okay for you to fuck up?"

"You're not even listening, Messiah. All you care about is how I hurt you. You're not even listening to all the pain you brought me."

"I hear everything you're saying, Julani. I understand that I hurt you, but I can't acknowledge it because when I do, I will feel your pain. We are one, Julani. I feel all the pain that you are going through. Tell me, can you feel mine?"

"Yes, I can feel your pain, which is the only reason I came to meet you today. I honestly just want to be left alone. I want to change my ways and I can't do that if you keep calling me. After this, I don't expect to hear from you again unless it has something to do with the baby. I just can't do the back and forth thing."

"That's cute ma," I laughed. "You think I'm just going to leave you alone so you can be with that nigga? Ma, the only life you will live is with me. I'll kill you first before I allow any other dude to be with you." Her body tensed up at the mention of death. I wouldn't really kill Julani, but I needed her to know that I was serious.

"Messiah, all I can is that I'm sorry. If the baby isn't yours, then you don't have to worry about me. Whenever you have to do business with my father, I'll make sure that I'm not home. I will make sure that I stay out of your way, but don't say you're going to kill me, Messiah. You have a whole other baby on the way with Amara. You need to live for her and your unborn child Messiah. Don't let my fuck ups be the reason you start behaving irrationally," she pleaded.

"But Amara is not you. I know I've done some fucked up shit Julani, but through it all, my love for you was real ma. It was real. You're all I see. You're my rainbow once the rain clears. Of course, I'm going to take care of the child I'm having with Amara, but with you is where I want to be," I sighed.

"No, I'm not Amara, and that's what attracted you to me in the first place. I was something new and different, trust me, I understand. But you see how you say it *was* real, that's past tense, meaning the love you once had for me is no longer there. The love I have for you is real Messiah, and it's killing me that I can't be with you. As much as it kills me, I know with you isn't where I need to be."

"We can be together, Julani. It can be just me and you. I just need you to give me one more chance. I promise you I won't fuck it up this time." I felt as if I was pleading for my life and it was falling on deaf ears.

"No, it can't because the two of us are not meant to be together. It wasn't written in the universe for us, which is why we had so much drama. Instead of listening, we kept trying to fight what we already knew, and in the process, we ended up hurting people who didn't deserve it."

"You're just trying to be with that nigga. He can't do shit for you though, Julani. He can't be the nigga that you need in your life. He don't even compare to the dude that I am."

"That's the thing, neither one of you can be the dude I need in my life because I don't need nor want a dude in my life. The only man that needs to be in my life is my father."

"I don't want to hear that shit Julani. You're mine or no one's at all," I spat and jumped out of her car.

I was losing my mind and she was the one to blame. I was partially to blame, but the majority of this shit was her fault. All I wanted was for us to be a family, but she didn't want to hear it. She probably took what I was saying as a joke, but I was dead ass serious. Despite what Julani thought, her and I were made for each other, we completed each other. For now, I was going to fall back until she came to her senses. I needed to get out of town and away from all the drama. I supplied some niggas up state with some work, so that's where I was headed. By the time I came back, Julani better have been ready to work things out. If she wasn't, I was gonna have to pull the trigger, and that was something I didn't want to do. However, if it needed to be done, then I would.

Chapter 6: Julani

It has been about two weeks since I had that horrible ass nightmare and everything has been on the up and up. My father was due home in another week, and I couldn't have been happier. Being in this big ass house alone was lonely as hell and I was in the house more often than I would've liked. The only time I went out was to go to the club to oversee a couple of things, or when Phallyn wanted to go shopping or out to eat and my doctor's appointments. Other than that, I was a home body. Baking ended up being a new hobby of mine, thanks to me watching *Cupcake Wars*. I would bake all kinds of different cupcakes, just to give me something to do. I would usually have Phallyn be my taste tester, but she complained about me making her fat.

So now that she no longer wanted to help me, I decided to call Cree over. In the past two weeks, Cree has really been the best friend that a woman could ask for in a man. He would text me every morning, call in the afternoon, and call at night, just to make sure I was okay. The attention he was showing me was very platonic and I loved it. There was no flirting or anything like that. He would ask me about the baby and make sure that I was eating. It felt good just to have a man in my life that was attentive to me. There was no sexual pressure between us, which made everything a lot smoother. He was definitely someone that I cherished to still have in my life.

Since the day Messiah and I met up at IHOP, I haven't heard from him. I wasn't really interested in him because of the threat. Did I think he would really kill me? No, but there was a possibility, and I didn't want to find out my odds. While I would handle business over the phone for my father, I would ask if anyone had seen him around, and everyone would say no. After the first couple of days of not hearing from him, I started sending him texts, trying to find out if he was okay or not. I was worried about him, but not worried enough to pop up at his home to see if he was good. Even though he told me him and Amara were done, I didn't want to chance showing up and her being there. Drama from her was the last thing I needed.

It hurt that Messiah couldn't put his issues aside that he had with me to be there for the baby that could possibly be his. However, I wasn't going to dwell on the situation either. When people go through things, it takes time for them to heal, and Messiah needed more than a little bit of time.

As I was taking my Oreo cupcakes out the oven, I heard a knock at the door. I looked at the security screen before going to the door. I saw it was Cree and with a smile on my face, I rushed over to the door, opening it.

"Damn Juju, you that happy to see a nigga," he laughed, walking in the door. He gave me a quick hug and a kiss on the cheek.

"I'm not happy to see you, I'm happy for you to taste these cupcakes I made." I closed the door behind him and walked into the kitchen.

"They smell good as shit. I hope you're not trying to kill me. You know they say the sweetest things are also the deadliest."

"Cree, why would I want to kill my maybe baby daddy?" I joked. I had to joke about the situation because if I didn't, I would probably cry. As time went on, I thought about my mistakes less, but when they would creep up, it would be hard for me to deal with.

"Ain't no maybe. That's my child, whether he or she has my DNA or not, and that's real shit Juju," he said, shocking the shit out of me.

I had no response for what he just said, so I didn't say anything. I popped the cupcakes out the pan and set them on a plate. I pulled everything I needed out the fridge and the cabinets to make my Oreo frosting, and got busy doing so. I could feel Cree staring at me, but I just refused to look. I thought it was cute that he was willing to claim my child whether it was really his or not. My thing was, if I chose not to be with him, would he still claim my child?

"Julani, I know you heard what I said, but I'm going to let you play deaf for the moment."

"Cree, what do you want me to say? Do I appreciate what you said? Yes, I do, but I don't know how to respond to that. For all I know, you're only saying that because you want me to be with you in the end."

"The fuck I look like saying that shit just to get with you. Julani, you bad, but you're not that fucking bad, so don't play yourself. I said what I said because it's the truth. That baby you're carrying is mine, regardless of any test. That's real shit. I'm not trying to game you because there is no need for that. I'm a stand up dude that does stand up things. It's as simple as that."

"Okay," was all I could think to say as I continued mixing the ingredients for my frosting.

"When the baby comes, are you going to stay here or do you want to get your own place?" Cree asked, moving the conversation along, and I was happy that he did.

"I'm not sure. I mean I think I should get my own place, but I'm not sure yet. I think I should talk to my father about it first."

"Julani, you are twenty-one, what are you asking your father for? You are about to be a mother. Are you going to ask your father if you should go out and get pampers when you only have two left?"

"No, but I think moving into my own place is something I should have a conversation with him about. I'm his only child and we are close," I shrugged.

"I understand all of that, but a part of growing up is you standing on your own two feet, and picking yourself up when you fall. Of course, he will always be there, but sometimes you have to do it on your own."

I thought about what he was saying and it all made sense. I kept saying how I wanted to grow up and stuff like that, but the first chance I get to make a grown up decision, I say I have to talk to my father first.

"I'm not trying to upset you or anything like that, I'm just trying to make sure you're good on all aspects."

"I understand what you're saying and you're right."

"Ight, now hurry up with them cupcakes because a nigga is hungry. Since baking is all you can do, I need to rack up on cupcakes."

"Wait, hold up, who said baking is the only thing that I can do? I throw down in the kitchen," I smiled.

"Oh, is that so?" he chuckled lightly.

"Yes, it's very much so." I was a little offended that he thought I couldn't cook. It was okay though because I was going to prove his ass wrong.

"Ight then, make me dinner while you're at it, since it's too late for lunch. I plan on chilling with you for the rest of the day anyway," he laughed.

"Oh, you think you are so slick, but I got you. Never underestimate Julani Marie Cortez," I giggled.

"Nah, I don't think I'm slick, I just know what I'm doing. When's your next doctor's appointment, and when do we get to find out what we are having?"

"I go back at the end of the month and we won't find out what I'm having until I'm five months. We still got three and a half months to go."

Just as I started frosting the cupcakes, Cree stuck his finger in the bowl and then placed his finger in his mouth.

"Don't look at me like that, I told you I was hungry as hell. That frosting is the shit though ma," he smiled.

He stuck his finger back in the bowl and came over to where I was. He spun me around, making me face him. Wiping the frosting on my lips, my body froze, not knowing what was going to happen next. Cree brought his lips to mine and gently licked and sucked the frosting off my lips. My body shivered from the pleasure I just received. This pregnancy was making me horny as hell, but I refused to have sex while not knowing whose child I was carrying. Before things got too hot and heavy, I attempted to push Cree away, but his hands clung to my hips.

"Cree, no," I moaned softly.

"You're saying no, but your body is calling me ma. I just want a kiss. I promise it won't go any further than that. Your lips are too juicy for me to pass up on," he moaned against my lips. I slipped my tongue into his mouth, giving in to my body's urges.

His hands slipped from my hips to my ass and I loved the way his hands felt feeling on my booty. The kiss that we were sharing wasn't a regular kiss. This kiss was so much more. I felt like we were sharing our true feelings for each other in the form of a kiss. The kiss was orgasmic; it was taking me to new heights.

"Damn," Cree said, pulling away, ending the kiss. I was glad he pulled away because I was almost ready to give him all of this good loving.

"Umm, you can take this cupcake and go watch TV in the living room, while I find something to cook. Are you allergic to anything?" I asked, stumbling over some of my words.

"Nah, I'm good, I just don't eat pork." He kissed me on the cheek, grabbed the cupcake and left out the kitchen.

I grabbed my chest, trying to steady my breathing. My hormones were on ten and I was ready to bust it open. I stuffed a cupcake in my mouth to stop a moan from escaping my lips. The cupcake tasted like heaven and did nothing because a moan still escaped my mouth. I laughed a little because I was all hot and bothered from a fucking kiss. A damn kiss had me acting a fool. I shook my head, but couldn't help but to think when a kiss is that damn good, that's how you know it's real.

* * * *

"I can't even clown you Juju, that food was good as hell," Cree smiled, downing his cup of soda. After getting myself together, I chose to make pepper steak, rice and beans, with a baked potato on the side.

"I would hope the food was good after watching you eat two and a half plates," I giggled.

"I told your ass I was hungry as hell, but you did your thing ma."

"Thank you. I don't know why you would think I couldn't cook. I throw down in the kitchen," I boasted. "Let me clean up the kitchen, then I will walk you out."

"You're trying to kick me out already? What if I told you I'm trying to spend the night?" I stopped doing what I was doing to look at him. I was so used to our new friendship, that all the flirting that was going on was taking me by surprise.

"Cree, that kiss was already too much. I'm not trying to do anything with you. We are just supposed to be friends, remember?"

"No one is trying to get in your draws. I just want to stay here with you to make sure you're good. You know, you bring up us just being friends a lot. You got me starting to think that you want to be more than friends. I mean, I'm still available, but a nigga like me won't be around for long. Shit, I'm a hot commodity." He started laughing and I joined in because Cree was honestly something else.

"Cree, if another girl wants to take you off my hands, then she has my blessings."

"Damn, it's like that Julani? You not feeling a nigga anymore?"

"Stop being so emotional, but why wouldn't I be good? I have lived in this house for the majority of my life," I sassed.

"I'm not saying you wouldn't be good. This is a big ass house; I know it can get lonely. I'm sure you have a guest bedroom I could sleep in, but if you scared you might let me have you, then it's cool. Just make me a to go plate and I'll be out your hair."

"I'm not worried about you having me because it's not even going down like that. I keep telling you we are strictly friends, and that's exactly what I mean. I guess you can sleep in one of the guest rooms, just make sure you don't end up in my bed." Cree was right, staying in this house was lonely as hell, and I really enjoyed his company.

"Ight, I'ma go back to my crib and get some clothes, then I'll be back. Have a movie ready or some shit."

"Okay," I smiled, watching him leave out the kitchen.

I started to clean up, putting all the dishes in the sink, when I heard him call out to me. I looked at the security camera and saw that Amara was standing at my door. *What the hell does she want?* I put down the dishes I had in my hand and went towards the front door. I hoped she wasn't trying to bring drama to my house because I wasn't here for it. I got to the door and my eyes fell right on her stomach. Hers was poking out more than mine, so I naturally assumed she was further along than I was. It shouldn't have bothered me that she was pregnant, but it did. I couldn't tear my eyes away from her stomach. The hurt I was feeling paralyzed my body. I wanted nothing more than to reach out and wring her neck, but I was better than that.

"Juju, you good or you need me to say?" Cree asked.

"And if she's not good, what the hell are you going to do, hit a pregnant woman?" Amara sassed.

The sound of her voice helped me remove my eyes from her stomach. I looked up, looking her in the face, and she looked like shit. Her hair was disheveled and thrown on the top of her head. Her eyes were puffy and red, making it look as if she'd been crying for the past week straight. Her attire was nowhere up to par like it usually is. She had on a pair of sweats, a t-shirt and some flip flops. This was definitely not the Amara I knew.

"Uh yeah, I will be fine," I told Cree. He kissed me on the cheek, looked at Amara, then left out.

"So, what are you doing here Amara? Last time we had a conversation, it didn't end well. I finally have some peace in my life and I would love to keep it that way." I was standing in the door because she wasn't about to come into my house. Whatever she needed to say could be said at my doorstep.

"I see that since you can't have Messiah, you moved on to the next. Is he your child's father or is there another guy that you have to get tested?" she giggled like she really said something funny.

"I will give you your props because he's cute, maybe I should try to steal him the way you did Messiah. I think that would be some good pay back, don't you?" she smirked. I promise I wanted to smack that smirk off her face. She was lucky both of us were pregnant because I would have pounced on her ass the minute she stepped foot on my property.

"Amara, what do you want? You came to my house and I'm not going to let you disrespect me at my house. Now say whatever it is that needs to be said before I slam the door in your face."

"That nasty attitude is the same reason Messiah didn't want to be with you. You thought because you were young, fresh and new, that he was just going to chase after you. Well you guessed wrong. Anyway, I came over to see if Messiah was here, but for obvious reasons, I know now that he's not."

"Wait, you came over here looking for Messiah? Why would Messiah be here? I haven't talked to him since the day after he kicked me out his house."

"He liked running back to trash in the past and I know old habits die hard. Since me and him are going through the motions, I figured he would run back to the trash."

"You have a smart mouth for someone who looks like shit," I told her. She was popping all this shit while looking like she hadn't bathed in days.

"I can talk all the shit I want to because I have a mouth. Everything that is going on in my life is your fucking fault."

"How is it my fault that you look like the trash you are?" I snapped.

"Don't play dumb, Julani. You knew Messiah had a bitch at home, but you still opened your legs like the hoe you are. You would think being King's daughter, you would have more self-respect. Messiah and I were good until your raggedy ass came along." I had to stop her right there because everything that happened wasn't just my fault.

"Let me stop you for a second because if you and Messiah were all good, then he wouldn't have been so willing. Trust me, he was willing and ready to get all of this," I rubbed my hands over my body for emphasis.

"You and Messiah have been together for years and he didn't wife your ass up. I'm sure there was a reason that he didn't. Just because the problems the two of you had weren't at the forefront, didn't mean they didn't exist. If you ask me, I did your fucking ass a favor."

"Bitch, you wish you did me a favor. I pray that Messiah isn't the father to your child."

"Going back and forth with you isn't going to get me anywhere. Messiah isn't here and I already apologized, so I'm not going to keep saying sorry to feed your ego. If you can't accept the apology, then that is your business. What you need to do is step before I forget that you're pregnant and beat that ass." I was tired of the insults because it wasn't doing anything for Amara, and it damn sure wasn't doing anything for me.

"I am going to leave because I have to go and find *my* baby father. Just remember what goes around, comes around."

"Yeah whatever, bye bitch," I mushed her, then slammed the door in her face.

I went back in the kitchen to finish cleaning up. I sighed a little because this was too much. All this time I thought Messiah was at home, and he was just ignoring everyone. I was worried about Messiah, even though I shouldn't have been, but how could I not. I was going to put in a few phone calls so he would be found. It was the least I could do after I drove him to disappear.

Amara showing up at my house unexpected showed me that she was going to be a problem. While I was ready to let go of all the drama that has been going on, it seemed like everyone else wanted to still hold on to it. I wasn't for all the petty drama anymore because I was going to be a mom in a few months. However, if Amara kept showing up, her ass was going to make me revert back to my old ways. Changed or not, she could get this work.

Chapter 7: Messiah

"Man, you need to chill out," Rich said.

"Nigga, I paid you for the shit, so give me what the fuck I came here for."

"You right, but don't ever say I didn't try to help your junkie ass," Rich spat. He threw the eight ball at me and stormed away. I caught it in midair and a smile spread on my face.

"Nigga, remember the reason you are getting money is because of me," I spat.

I quickly left out of the trap house and went back over to my car. I didn't even bother driving off. Shit, I didn't even give a fuck who saw me. I pulled out a magazine I had in the glove compartment, and sat it on my lap. Pouring the white substance on the magazine, I created a line. My eyes lit up at the sight of my drug of choice. I leaned forward, sniffing it, going into a whole different universe. My eyes rolled a little as I sat there trying to gather myself.

Yeah, a nigga was doing coke, but so the fuck what. This was the only thing that was helping me cope with being without Julani. I quickly did another line, then put my stash under the passenger's seat. I drove back to the hotel I was staying at, feeling high as a kite. The drugs were the only thing that were keeping me sane. After talking to Julani, I went home to pack up enough shit that would last me a week. I took some money with me and got ghost. I didn't say anything to Amara because I only planned on being gone a week.

When I first got to the hotel, I was cool. I planned on staying in my room and just chilling out. For the first two days it was cool, but on the third day, that's when things took a turn for the worse. There was a crazy hotel party going on in the suite next to me. They invited me, and of course I went. I walked in the room and was the only black person there. I didn't feel uncomfortable because I was that nigga. To make a long story short, I smoked a couple of blunts that were laced with coke. I didn't think nothing of it because I didn't think I would get hooked that quick.

The joke was on me because the next day, my body craved it. I tried to fight the urge, but then images of Julani sleeping with that other nigga began to pop in my head. I saw them and my child living happily ever after. It went as far as Julani marrying the nigga, and that was when I couldn't take it anymore. I rode out to the trap my nigga Rich worked out of and copped some. It was only supposed to be that one time, but one time turned into two, two turned into three and after the tenth time, I lost count. The week I was supposed to be out here, turned into two, and I didn't have any intensions of leaving anytime soon.

I couldn't face reality and I damn sure couldn't face Julani being with that nigga. So I planned on staying here where Julani and I were together. Julani would text me asking me was I okay and keeping me up to date with the baby, but I just couldn't bring myself to reply while I was in this mind state. When I got high, I saw my future. I saw my future with Julani. Instead of her marrying that corny nigga, she married me. The child she was carrying was a boy, and life was perfect. But as soon as the high wore off, it was back to Julani being with dude.

I was getting low on money, so I would have to leave and go back home soon. By the time I got on E, I needed to have a plan in motion for me to get Julani. I didn't want to hurt her, I just wanted her to come back with me. We could build a whole new life in Mount Vernon. Mount Vernon could be our new kingdom that we could rule with an iron fist. It would just be me and her, and whoever tried to get in the way of us being together would have to die.

"Fuck, what about Amara?" I question out loud.

"I guess I could leave her behind," I answered.

There was no way I could take Amara and Julani, so I made a choice to just take Julani. That's who I really wanted to be with anyway. I would just have to come back for my child once Julani and I were settled. I'm sure Amara would understand. I had to go after what I loved the most and that was Julani. Nothing compared to her. The coke was my high, but she took me even higher. I pulled up to the hotel and did a couple more lines. I leaned my head back, feeling as if I was on cloud nine. Yeah, my mind was made up; I was going to go back and get my bitch. It was Julani and I until death do us part.

Chapter 8: Julani

"Julani! Julani!" I popped up out of bed to the sound of my father's voice.

"Juju, what you doing? It's too early, lay back down," Cree groaned, trying to pull me back in the bed.

When Cree came back yesterday, we chilled and watched movies like we planned on doing. However, when it got time for us to go to sleep, he somehow ended up in my bedroom, instead of one of the guest rooms. We didn't do anything, but I did appreciate his body being snuggled up to mine. I was missing affection, and he filled the void for that night.

"Cree, no, you have to get up. I think I heard my father," I said, pushing him, trying to wake him up.

"Ight, chill out," he yawned, sitting up in the bed.

I got out of bed, slipped my feet into my slippers and ran downstairs. My father wasn't supposed to be home yet; he was supposed to be gone for a couple more weeks.

"Daddy, what are you doing here?" I asked once I saw him at the bottom of the stairs.

"I don't get a hug or nothing?" he asked, looking at me funny. I giggled and ran into his arms. I didn't care how old I was, I loved my father to death. I would forever be a daddy's girl.

"That's more like it. I came home early because I couldn't leave you alone, pregnant and all."

"Daddy, you don't have to worry about me, I'm good. I got myself into this mess and I will be the one to get myself out."

"Julani, you never have to deal with anything alone as long as I have air in my lungs."

"I know daddy, but you can't fix every situation I mess up. At some point, I have to take responsibility for my actions, and me being pregnant is where I'm going to start."

"Where is Julani Marie Cortez because you aren't her," my father laughed.

"This is me, or should I say the new me. Something has finally got through this thick skull of mine. I plan on being the grown woman that you raised me to be."

"I'm happy to hear that, but I'm always here for you when you need me. Now how is Messiah taking the news?"

While my father was away, I told him I was pregnant, I just didn't tell him there was a possibility of two men being the father. I wanted to tell him that face to face because I knew he was going to be pissed.

"Umm, I haven't really seen Messiah, he is missing. I made some calls yesterday, but I haven't heard anything back from anyone."

"Why the fuck would he disappear when he knows you're pregnant? That nigga gonna make me put my foot up his ass. I didn't want him fucking with you in the first place and this was exactly why."

"You can't blame him for disappearing because it is partially my fault."

"Don't tell me you pushed him away because he wouldn't be with you Julani. I taught you better than that. If he doesn't want to be with you, then let his ass fucking go."

"What are you talking about? I don't care if he wants to be with me or not because I'm over him and that whole situation. He disappeared because there is a possibility he may not be the father. Cree may be the father to my child."

As if on cue, at the mention of his name, Cree walked into the living room.

"Wassup Mr. Cortez?" Cree greeted him. "Julani, come walk me out right quick."

I looked at my father and he nodded his head, telling me to go. I got up, nervous as hell, because my father ignored Cree's greeting and he wore a blank facial expression. My father was usually easy to read, but not this time.

"Are you going to call me later?" Cree asked when we got to the door.

"Probably not because I have to deal with my father and a couple of other things," I told him.

"You know if you just let me be there for you the way I'm trying to, you wouldn't have to go through this alone. I already told you fuck a DNA, that's my child."

"And I already told you that I just want to be friends," I sighed.

"You don't need a friend right now. You need a man in your life that's going to make you better. That whole focusing on myself thing is good, but you can do that while I'm looking out for all three of us. Ma, you can fight it all you want, but us being together is destined to be."

"If it's destined to be, then you can wait these months out."

"Ight, you got it ma." He kissed my cheek, then walked out of the door. Cree was right, the chemistry between the two of us was amazing, but I was serious about not wanting to date right now. I walked back in the living room to finish having the conversation with my father. As soon as I sat down, my father started to chew my ass out.

"Julani, how the hell did you end up not knowing who your child's father is? Matter of fact, don't even answer that. I raised you better than that Julani. Do you know how much hurt and pain you are causing both of those guys?"

"Yes, I understand that I'm causing them pain, but there is nothing I can do about. They both know about the other and it's their choice whether they want to go through this pregnancy with me or not. I'm not twisting any arms because I'm willing and ready to do this on my own."

"Man, Julani this shit is crazy," my father expressed, running his hand down his face.

"Daddy, I already know, but I'm handling this the best way that I know how. I told both of them that I didn't want to be in a relationship with either one of them because I wanted to take time out to focus on becoming a better person."

"Then what's Cree doing here?"

"He stayed the night with me because he didn't want me in this big ass house alone. You can't fault him for that."

"I'm going to keep my opinion about this situation to myself because you are a grown woman and I can't come to your rescue all the time. What I will say is I don't want Cree nor Messiah spending the night in my house."

"Okay, no problem," I told him.

"Ight, I'm going upstairs to take a nap because all this shit is stressing me out. Before I go, I want to say that I'm proud of you Julani. I'm not happy about the situation you got yourself in, but I am proud of how you are dealing with it. A lot of girls would be out acting a fool instead of trying to be better for their child."

"Thank you daddy."

I watched him walk up the stairs and let out a sigh of relief. The conversation went a lot better than I expected it to. I expected this to be the last time that my behavior would be brought up. I was tired of people bringing it up when it was in the past. I wasn't looking back anymore after today. I planned on looking forward because I was already at my lowest; the only place to go from here is up.

Chapter 9: Cree

I thought the nine months Julani was pregnant was going to be long as hell. Instead of them dragging, they flew by. The months were flying by in a blink of an eye. The closer it got to her due date, the more nervous I became. I know I said regardless of this child being mine or not, I would be there for Julani, and that was the truth, but a part of me would be crushed if the baby wasn't mine. I wouldn't love the baby any less, it would just hurt. A nigga was going to man up though for the sake of Julani.

She was already five months and it was time to find out the sex of the baby. I was excited as hell and I'm sure Julani was too. All she talked about was finding out the sex so she could go shopping and shit. I didn't care what the sex was because either way, I was putting them in boxing classes. My child was going to know how to throw them blows, amongst other things.

I sat in the car, watching Julani zip up her jacket all the way. This winter was something serious. The cold winter chill wasn't playing with anyone this year. She waddled into the doctor's office with a smile on her face. I figured she was ready to find out the sex. We have talked about it on numerous occasions and she said she wanted a boy. Her reason was because she didn't want a girl that acted like her. I had to reassure her that if she had a girl, everything would be fine because she would be taught everything she needs to know by the sweetest woman in the world.

I waited a couple of seconds before getting out my car and going inside. The reason I let her go in first was because I didn't want her to know that I was just as anxious as her. I wanted to play it cool because I still wasn't sure where we stood. She was still claiming that we were just friends, but I was over that whole thing. She was five months and now was the time to establish if there was going to be a relationship between the two of us.

I walked in and briefly looked around the room for where Julani was sitting. When our eyes connected, she waved her hand and I walked towards her. The further along in her pregnancy she got, the hornier she got. She thought I didn't know it, but all the sexual thoughts she was having right now, were displayed on her face.

"Stop looking at me like that before I put this dick in your life," I smirked. I leaned down, kissing her on the cheek. I wanted Juju in the worse way, but I was going to wait for her to make the first move.

"Nobody wants what you have to offer. After being pregnant, I may just become a born again virgin and wait until I'm married to have sex." Thinking it was a joke, I laughed. The look on her face let me know she was somewhat serious about the situation.

"Oh, you're serious, my bad Julani. What makes you want to become a born again virgin?"

"Sex got me into all this mess and I'm not trying to be stuck in another situation like this again. The next person I give myself to, I want them to be my husband."

"You don't think this nine month wait you got me on is long enough?"

"Who said I'm going to let you hit after I have this baby?"

"Nobody has to say it because your body does that for you. I know you want me and you know it too. The sooner you admit it, the sooner we can get everything popping. Ma, the ball is in your court, I'm just waiting for you to take the shot."

"If I wanted you, I would have you. All I have to do is say the word and you will be mine," she purred. I waved her ass off because she was doing nothing but playing games, which was what she did best.

"Yeah whatever, Juju. I hear that hot shit you're talking," I laughed. "On a serious note, I need to talk to you about something serious."

"I already told you that I'm not dating anyone Cree. I wish you would stop bringing it up," she sighed. I looked at her like she was crazy. For the past three months, I have been pressuring her about making things official, because if you ask me, we were dating, just without a title. I didn't give a fuck about a title, I just needed her to admit it. I needed her to admit to herself that her feelings for me were true. I wasn't one of these little niggas running around. I knew what I wanted and I wasn't scared to say it. I needed the same thing in return from her.

"Juju, you're already mine, so that shit you just said is irrelevant.

"Then why do you keep bringing it up then?"

"I didn't bring it up, you did. I wasn't trying to talk to you about that shit. I need to talk to you about your boy."

"Who's my boy?" she asked confused.

"Messiah," I kept it short. Since Messiah disappeared, Julani has been stressing about the nigga. Every time I asked her about him, she would try to act like she didn't care, but I knew better. I knew her better, so I looked into the nigga's whereabouts.

"What about him?" she asked. I swear to you not, it was like I could hear her heart beating out of her chest. That right there told me that the feelings she had for Messiah were still there. I wasn't upset or nothing because I expected them to be there. They had history, so I could respect it. Now if she acted on them, then that would be a whole different story.

"I had my people look into him disappearing and shit because I know it has been fucking with you. My people found him out in Mount Vernon."

"Okay, so he's good, right?" her voice was calm, but that was about the only thing that was. She was shaking her leg, anticipating my answer. I knew the next thing that was about to come out my mouth was going to hurt her. I tried to pick my words wisely because I wanted to cause her the least bit of pain possible.

"The dude isn't dead, so I guess he's straight," I began, but she cut me off.

"Then if he isn't dead, what's wrong with him?"

"The nigga is hooked on that white," I told her.

"When you say that white, do you mean coke or heroin?" she asked with panic evident in her eyes.

"He's smoking coke. My dudes say he was tripping big time." She turned away from like she didn't want me to see the hurt on her face.

"Julani, don't turn your head away from me because you don't want me to see you're hurt. I understand, trust me I understand. I don't fault you for still caring about dude. That's the whole reason I went to look for him," I whispered, cupping her chin.

"This is all my fault," she whispered back.

"You can't blame yourself for that man's actions," I tried to explain, but the nurse came out from the back.

"Julani Cortez," the nurse called out.

"I'm here," Julani said back.

I wiped the tears that managed to slip down her face, before we got up and walked to the back. I held her hand, letting her know I was here for her if she needed me. The rest of the appointment was a blur for both of us. Julani was answering all the doctor's questions, but she wasn't really there. My mind was on Julani hurting. I could have been selfish and got mad about her caring about Messiah, but that wasn't even important right now. The fact that she was hurting was the only thing on my mind. I think the only thing both of us paid attention to was the doctor telling us the sex of the baby. We were having a boy and I couldn't have been happier.

"You sure you're okay to drive ma?" I asked when we left out the hospital. She was still in a daze and I didn't think it would be good for her to drive.

"Yeah, I'm fine," she told me, lying.

"Julani, when are you going to learn that you can't lie to me. I know you better than I know myself, so stop with that fucking lying shit. You are not fine. Your ass is in a daze right now. Let me drive you home," I offered.

"No!" she screamed out. "I mean, no, you don't have to drive me home. I'll call Phallyn and have her come get me. I'm not in the mood to be in the house anyway."

"Ight, well I'm going to wait with you until she gets here. Get in the car, it's too cold for you to be standing out here."

She jumped in the driver's seat before I could, and instead of arguing with her, I just let her rock. I watched her pull out her phone and call Phallyn. She said a couple of words, then hung up the phone.

"Phallyn is only ten minutes away. She's going to walk over here and ride with me home," she told me with a faint smile.

"Ight. Julani, if you want to talk about Messiah, just let me know and I'll be the shoulder you need to cry on."

"I need you to tell me exactly where you found Messiah," she said.

"For what?" I questioned. I know she wasn't about to do what I think she was going to do.

"It doesn't matter for what, I just need to know where you found him," she snapped.

"Julani, I'm not letting you go up to Mount Vernon to save that nigga. I found him for you because I knew you were worried about the nigga. The fuck I look like letting my girl go run after another dude." Now I was starting to get pissed. Messiah was a grown ass man and he was doing exactly what he wanted to do. Julani needed to stop allowing Messiah to pull her back in.

"First of all, I'm not your girl, so I can go run after whoever I want to. You're just mad I'm not running after you. You probably thought telling me about Messiah's drug problem was going to give you a better chance at being with me. Well guess what, you thought wrong. I'm going to find out where Messiah is because he needs me right now. I'm sure if the roles were reversed, you would want me to come and save you."

"Nah, if the roles were reversed, you wouldn't have to worry about me needing you to save me because I would be man enough to save my damn self. I get it now, so you don't have to worry about a nigga anymore. I'm all the way straight on you, and that's word to," I laughed lightly to keep from spazzing the fuck out on her.

"What is that supposed to mean?" she had the nerve to ask.

"It means exactly what it sounds like. I'm tired of kissing your ass and trying to be there for you when you obviously don't want me around. I'm no longer gonna be your lost little puppy, ma. You can do whatever you need to do, Juju."

"You're just mad because I won't make things official with you."

"It's not even about that and that's how I know I need to leave your ass alone. I'm over here putting in work for us and you're ready to run behind a nigga that just fucking up and left you when he knows you might be carrying his baby. Not to mention, he's not even fucking with his other baby mama. That's the type of nigga you want, Julani? You want a nigga that don't give a fuck about the two who are having his kids? If that's the type of dude you want to be with, then who am I to stand in your way."

"Cree, you are blowing things way out of proportion. It was okay for you to go find him, but I can't go help him? What kind of ass backwards shit is that?"

"I went to go find him off the strength of you and that's it. But I'm good on you, so I don't need to explain myself. Phallyn is finally here, so you can go do what the fuck you need to do," I spat, getting out the car.

Phallyn jumped in the car as Julani and I had a staring contest. I broke the stare off and headed back towards my car. I was tired of playing these games with Julani. Her and Messiah were stuck in this never ending circle, and I was tired of trying to pull Julani out. If she wanted to be with that nigga, then so be it, but I was done with her. The only thing I needed to know was if the baby she was carrying was mine.

Chapter 10: Julani

"Julani, I'm going to need you to explain what the hell is going on? And slow the hell down before you kill us both," Phallyn sassed.

"I need to find out where in Mount Vernon Messiah is. Cree told me that he's out there doing drugs and shit." The shit didn't even sound right when I said it out loud. There was no way this shit drove Messiah to do drugs. Cree had to be lying, so I would forget all about Messiah and move on with him. Yeah, Cree was lying, Messiah wasn't doing no drugs. His actions back there showed me exactly the type of person he was. As long as he was happy, nobody else mattered. I liked him because he was so mature, but how could someone so mature not want me to help someone who was in need?

"No, you're fucking lying. Messiah isn't on no damn drugs." The way Phallyn said it, made it come out more as a question, than a statement.

"Don't even question that shit because it's not true. Messiah is a street nigga and he knows the first rule is never get high off your own supply. Cree has to be jealous or some shit." I was trying my hardest to convince myself that this was a lie because if it was the truth, I wouldn't be able to handle it. I was having a boy and his possible father might be on drugs. If this wasn't karma for my ass, I didn't know what was.

"What would make Cree go looking for Messiah anyway?"

"He claims it was because he knew I was worried about Messiah. I don't believe that shit at all."

"Maybe he did do it out of the kindness of his heart. That boy is in love with you Julani, trust me, I know. I'm sure he just did it to look out for you. Shit, who knows, Messiah might really be on drugs."

"The fuck you mean he might really be on drugs? We both know Messiah, and doing drugs isn't his type of thing."

"There is no need to take your anger out on me. I did nothing to you. You don't know what Messiah is capable of because Messiah isn't the same dude he was when we were growing up. I'm sure you thought he would never break your heart and guess what, he did. I don't know why you're making it a big deal like him being on drugs is the worst thing in the world. At least his ass is high and not dead."

I couldn't believe the shit that was coming out of Phallyn's mouth. This was the reason we have been fighting so much lately. She is so insensitive and she says whatever she wants, without thinking about how the person would feel.

"Phallyn, I can't believe you just said that."

"Well believe it, because it's the truth. I can't give Messiah the benefit of the doubt because look at all the bullshit he has been up to. He knows you're pregnant, but his ass disappears. Shit, he isn't even there for Amara and they've been together for years. That right there should tell you something."

"He left because he couldn't handle the fact that the baby might not be his. Try putting yourself in his shoes, and then maybe you will understand." I was defending Messiah like my life depended on it. It was as if I was the only who could see the good in him. Everyone else just saw the Messiah who caused me so much hurt and pain.

"Cree is in the same situation that he is in, yet Cree is still by your side. All you're doing is making excuses for him and that isn't helping anyone. You say you're over him, but look how you're acting right now. You just found out the sex of your child, yet you are rushing to go find Messiah. I don't know how many times I have to tell you this, but you keep playing Cree to the side and you are going to miss out on a good thing."

"I'm so tired of hearing how Cree and I are supposed to be together. If you are so Team Cree, why don't you fuck him and go have a child? I'm a bad person because I'm concerned about my possible baby's father. All I'm trying to do is make things right for everyone, yet I end up on everyone's shit list."

No matter what I did, I couldn't keep both Cree and Messiah happy. I was supposed to be focusing on myself this pregnancy, but I somehow ended up worrying about everyone else.

"I'm not saying you're a bad person, but come on. Amara is his girl and she's not even out here looking for him anymore, that should tell you something. All I'm saying is that you can't always try to help Messiah or do what you feel is best for Messiah. We are supposed to be celebrating your five-month mark and yet you are worried about him. When are you going to see that all he does is pull you down with him? It's going to take something drastic for you to leave Messiah alone. It's sad to say, but that is the honest truth."

"Why would you wish something like that on me?"

"I'm not wishing anything on you. All I said is that it's going to take something drastic for you to realize that you need to leave Messiah alone. I thought the dream you had would have done it, but obviously it didn't. At some point, you have to put yourself first and stop worrying about everyone else."

"I know all of that Phallyn, but you just don't understand. What if Messiah is doing drugs because of me? What if I hurt him so bad he turned to drugs to cope with the pain? How am I supposed to live with myself knowing that I hurt someone so bad they wanted to damage their body? This could be his baby I'm carrying and I will have to explain to him why his father isn't around. You may not understand, and that's okay, but this is something that I'm going to do with or without you."

I pulled up to my house and jumped out of the car, leaving Phallyn behind. My father's car was in the driveway, causing me to waddle in the house faster. Cree didn't want to tell me where Messiah was, but I knew my father would. My father may not have been happy with Messiah's actions, but he still looked at him as a son.

"Daddy!" I yelled, walking into the house. I left the door open, just in case Phallyn was going to come in.

"Julani, what are you calling me for? Screaming like you done lost your damn mind. Did you find out the sex?" my father was talking, but he wasn't saying anything I wanted to hear. I rushed to the stairs and started climbing them as he was walking down.

"You couldn't wait for me to get to the bottom of the stairs?" he asked, eyeing me.

"Daddy, I need help finding Messiah. I found out he is in Mount Vernon and doing coke," I said it all in one breath because I didn't think I was going to be able to get it out.

"I know," my father said, then walked around me to finish walking down the stairs.

I watched him, trying to figure out what the hell just happened. I know he didn't just say I know. There was no way my father would just let Messiah do drugs. I went after him because I needed answers. If he did know about Messiah's drug problem, why wasn't he doing anything about it?

"Daddy, you can't just walk away from me like that after saying that you knew Messiah had a drug problem."

"Julani, what more do you want me to say?" he asked, sitting down on the couch.

"I want you to say more than what you are saying right now. If you knew, why didn't you try to help him out or something?"

"I can't help a man that doesn't want to be helped. Messiah is like a son to me, but it comes a point in time when you have to step away and allow him to grow up. I tried to help Messiah, but he didn't want the help I was offering. Him being a man, I had to respect it and hope that he would come to his senses. When the time is right, Messiah will come around and get help, but for now, there is nothing that can be done."

"What the hell you mean he didn't want your help? You should have made him accept your help daddy. We just can't leave him out there alone. He might be the father of my baby and he needs to be around," I whined.

"Julani! There is nothing that I can do, I already tried. When Messiah wants to come around, he will, but until then, the only thing we can do is pray for him."

"Ugh!" I yelled out.

I glared at my father before walking out of the house. I didn't want to hear what he had to say because it wasn't helping anything. I always looked to my father to make things better. He was my super hero, and whenever I had a problem, he came to my rescue. I may not have been in trouble, but Messiah was. I felt he still should've swooped in and saved him. When I got outside, Phallyn was still sitting in the car. I felt bad for the way I talked to her, but it seemed like when it came to Messiah, Phallyn was just anti him.

I walked over to the car, got in and drove away. I didn't have a destination in mind, I just drove until I ended up at the house Messiah shared with Amara. I didn't know what made me come here, but this is where I ended up.

"Julani, what are we doing here?" Phallyn asked me. I looked at her with sad eyes, shrugging my shoulders.

"Man Julani, you can't let what Messiah is going through effect you like this."

"I know, but I just need to know if she knows that Messiah is upstate doing drugs, while she's packing up to move. Like you said, Messiah and her have history; maybe she will be able to knock some sense into him."

"I'm letting you know now, this isn't a good idea, but if this is what you want to do, I'm right behind you," Phallyn said, getting out the car.

I was happy as hell that she decided to come with me. If I had to go to this door by myself, I didn't know how things were going to turn out. We walked up to the door and I knocked twice. Time passed and nothing. I knocked some more and this time, the door flew open.

"What the fuck are you doing here?" Amara asked, not bothering to hide the annoyance in her voice.

"I came to find out if you knew that Messiah was up in Mount Vernon doing coke."

Amara started laughing, causing Phallyn and I to step back a little. From the way she was laughing, you would think she hit a psychotic break or something.

"You're just now finding out about that shit? You are a little too late mama. I already know and I already got him. You see, his boys know of me, not you. When things go wrong, everyone knows to call me. They call because I'm the girlfriend, not you. I'm the girl that he claims in these streets, not you. You were just something to do when there was nothing to do. Now that you know *my* man is straight, you can remove yourself from my porch," she spat.

I have never been speechless before, until this moment. For some reason, what Amara said got to me. It shouldn't have, but it did. Here I was, trying to do the right thing yet again, and I was being read my rights. How many times am I going to keep putting myself through this?

"Bitch, don't talk to her like that. She only came over to put you up on game about your baby father. The least your raggedy ass could do is say thank you," Phallyn spat. I loved her because when I wasn't able to defend myself, she was there to do it for me.

"This has nothing to do with you."

"As long as it has to do with Julani, it will forever have something to do with me. The fuck are you so salty for? Are you mad because Julani was the only bitch to pull Messiah from your ass? You must feel threatened. Yeah, that's it, you're threatened because a young bitch came and showed you how it's done. Instead of being bitter, you should be taking notes."

"Taking notes on what? How to steal another chick's man? There is no point in taking notes on that because I don't have to steal another bitch's man because I can get my own," Amara began to go off, but Messiah came rushing to the door.

Our eyes locked; my heart didn't flutter or anything, instead of feeling love or pain, I felt disgust. Looking at Messiah was disgusting me right now.

"Julani!" he whispered.

"Messiah, you are not well enough to come outside."

"Bitch, get the fuck out of my way." I watched Messiah mush Amara out the way and I felt bad for her. She didn't deserve this shit, just like I didn't.

"Messiah, you didn't have to push her like that," I told him.

"She was stopping me from getting to you. You see what happens when someone stops me from getting to you Julani. I will do anything just to be in your presence. You're all I see, Julani."

"But she's pregnant," I told him.

"I understand that, but at the end of the day, you are who I want. Until I have you in my arms, no one else matters to me. I refuse to let anyone else fucking have you. Julani, I love you ma. You're my world, without you there is no sense in living."

This shit was like something out of the twilight zone. Messiah was confessing his love to me, but it did nothing for me. Amara was finally off the floor and standing by the door with tears in her eyes. Phallyn was just standing there, watching us with a look of pity on her face.

"Messiah, I can't do this with you. I'm glad you're semi okay, but I have to go," I told him. I couldn't stand here and deal with this shit anymore.

"Okay, you can go, but I will be coming for you soon. Just make sure you and my son are ready to go when it's time," he said smiling, while keeping his eyes trained on my stomach.

"How do you know it's a boy?" I asked.

"Don't worry about it, I just know. Phallyn, hurry up and get my wife home," he said, walking back towards the house, pulling Amara in and closing the door.

I looked at Phallyn as if to say what the fuck just happened, but she only shook her head. She grabbed my hand and led me back to my car. She got in the driver's seat, while I got in the passenger's. There was no way I was going to be able to drive with all this shit on my mind. From the way Messiah was acting, he had to be doing more than just coke.

The way he shoved Amara showed me all I needed to see. This time, I was honestly going to leave all things Messiah alone. I could no longer try to save him, because every time I tried, he would pull me down with him. At first, I claimed I wanted him around for the baby's sake, but that wasn't the truth. The truth was, I wanted Messiah around because I still wanted him to love me. I still wanted to be with him. Every time I said I no longer wanted Messiah, I was lying to myself. Me wanting Messiah was the reason I kept pushing the friendship thing with Cree. Cree was the dude I was supposed to be with, while Messiah was the bad boy I was told to stay away from. We were living like something out of an urban fiction book. The only difference was, I wasn't going to keep running after the dude that wasn't for me.

Chapter 11: Julani

Five days had gone by and I still refused to leave out of the house. I just didn't feel like dealing with anyone. I was supposed to be on this path of self-righteousness, but I somehow ended up getting caught up in Messiah's bullshit once again. I couldn't even blame him this time because this was all me. I allowed the love I still had for him to bring me back down the path I was trying to avoid. I was happy he was back at home. I hoped and prayed that he was no longer doing drugs, but I couldn't worry about that anymore. The whole time he was gone, my mind was going crazy not knowing that he was okay. I couldn't do that anymore.

Then I had Cree who has done nothing but been there for me, yet I still pushed him away. I felt like shit for the way I talked to him the day he told me Messiah was doing drugs. I didn't mean to spazz on him, but at the same time, I felt like he had an ulterior motive. I felt as though he was trying to throw Messiah's fucks ups in my face so that he could look like the right choice. Or maybe I was just trying to sabotage what me and him could possibly have. Being with Messiah would be easy because I already knew what to expect from him; Cree was new and different. I knew Cree, but at the same time, I didn't. Cree was a mystery and I wasn't sure if I wanted to solve it or not.

"Julani, I need you to get the hell out of this house. You have not left this house in the past five days and I'm tired of seeing you mope around this bitch as if your life is over," my father barked, barging into my room.

"You could have at least knocked or something. You're invading my privacy," I complained.

"You don't have no privacy when you live under my roof."

"Well thanks for letting me know." I rolled my eyes at him and got out of bed. I attempted to walk out the room, but he blocked my path. I looked up at him with questioning eyes. In all my years, I have never seen my father act like this.

"Sit down, Julani."

"I'm trying to get out the house like you just told me to do."

"I didn't ask for a smart ass remark, I told you to go sit down, so sit the fuck down. I have been trying to let you fix the mistakes you have made, but obviously I'm going to have to step in. Now sit the fuck down."

I pouted, but went and sat my ass back on my bed. I honestly didn't want to hear anything my father had to say. If he wanted me to fix my mistakes, then he should allow me to do so the way I see fit. Yeah, I messed up a little, but I was still somewhat on the right path.

"Look Julani, you really need to have an inner talk with yourself. I don't know who this person is that you've become, but I don't like her. The person you are now isn't the person I raised you to be. When I first came back from my trip, you told me you were going to focus on yourself. I had reservations about that, but I bit my tongue to see how you would handle things.

From what I can see, you kept things platonic with Cree, but as soon as Messiah is in need, you want to rush to his aid and for what? He has a woman that's in his life who can run to go help him. Who do you think I called when I found out Messiah was strung out? I called Amara, because Amara is his girl. I know to hear that hurts, but it's the truth. You and Messiah are not meant to be together and the sooner you understand that, the better off the both of y'all will be."

"Daddy, I hear everything you're saying, but you just don't understand. I know that Messiah and I aren't supposed to be together, but it's hard to not care about him. The feelings I have for him run deep."

"Julani, I know you heard everything I'm saying because you're not deaf. I need you to understand what I'm saying. There is a difference between hearing and understanding baby girl. I need you to understand that Messiah is not good for you and you're not good for him. The best thing either one of you could do is leave the other alone. You don't even need a nigga in your life right now. You need to be working on you and getting back to the young lady that I raised."

"I understand daddy." I did understand where my father was coming from and he was absolutely right.

"Actions speak louder than words. You need to show me that you understand. From now until you have that baby, I don't want to hear shit about you and Messiah. I'm going to let Messiah know the same thing. Focus on you, your child and business, Julani. Give my grandson a mother he can be proud of."

"I will daddy."

I gave my father a hug and told him I loved him. He told me he loved me back before letting me know he was going back out of town next week. He asked me did I want to go with him and I declined. If I were to go out of town, I would feel as if I was running away from my problems. I ran away from them enough. It was now time to face them head on. I was going to make my father proud and be the Julani that he raised me to be.

Chapter 12: Cree

Once again, Julani had chosen that bitch nigga over me. It has been about a week and a half since the day I told her about Messiah's drug problem. Shit, the only reason I looked into it was because I knew she was stressed out behind it. She wasn't going to admit it, but I knew Julani well enough to know when something was bothering her. I hoped telling her would give her ass a piece of mind, but that obviously wasn't the case. She took a turn for the worse and I didn't know how we were going to get back right after this shit.

"Nigga, are you listening to anything that I'm saying to your ass?" Jacori asked, pulling me out of my thoughts.

"Nigga, get your fucking hand out my face and shit." We were at my crib, chilling in my office. Earlier, we went over all of his numbers pertaining his business, and now we were just chilling.

"You need to get your head out of Julani's ass. She got your head all the way fucked up."

"Nigga, you not saying anything I don't already know. It's just something about her ass that pulls me to her, no matter how much I don't want to be with her."

"That's what that pussy does to niggas. They get you hooked line and sinker, then want to play with your fucking emotions. I'm happy Phallyn not on that bullshit. She all about her business for the most part. I'm trying to get her to move out to Atlanta with me."

"Oh word, y'all trying to makes moves like that?" I wasn't surprised because Phallyn and Jacori were inseparable. I want a love like theirs because they were down for each other and always talked shit out. With Julani, it was always games on top of games, and for a minute, I was down to play, but as of right now, I wasn't feeling the shit.

"Hell yeah, we trying to make moves like that, or at least I am. Whenever I bring that shit up, she tries to tell me how she can't leave Julani and all this bullshit. Trust me though, before the new year, we will be all packed and headed to the A. I'm ready to give up this drug shit anyway. The fuck am I still doing it for if a nigga got more money than he can spend."

"It's 'bout time. I would've thought your ass would've stopped years ago. This shit is for the birds, on the real." I was proud of Jacori 'cause this nigga has been selling that shit for as long as I can remember. He damn sure didn't need to keep doing it because he had more money than he could spend.

"Yeah, a nigga is growing up and shit, trying to settle down," he began to talk, but his sentence was cut off when my office door opened. Standing there with the prettiest smile I've ever seen, was Julani.

"You didn't have to push me Phallyn, how do you even know where his office is?" she sassed.

"That doesn't matter. Jacori, let me talk to you real quick," Phallyn said.

Jacori looked back at me and I nodded, letting him know it was cool to leave. My eyes wandered over Julani, but they landed on her stomach. There was a possibility that Messiah could've been the father, but I didn't believe that shit at all. That was my child causing Julani's glow.

"Hey Cree," Julani said nervously.

"Sit down and stop acting like you don't know a nigga BM."

"BM?" she questioned.

"Yeah, baby mother. But wassup, what you doing here? Did you find ole boy?"

"I came here to talk to you about a couple of things. Messiah isn't one of them, but to answer your question, yes, I found him. He was at Amara's house, but that was something I should have known."

"What you want to talk about tho?" I wanted her to get to the point because I wasn't really fucking with her like that.

"I came here to tell you that I don't want you around until after I have this baby. I appreciate how you have stuck by me this whole time, but I need to do this alone. I only have about four more months, so it's not even that long of a time. After having a talk with my father, I realized that I need to focus on me, and I can't do that while you are around."

"Fuck all that shit you talking Julani. You want me to stay away from you for the next four months like you're not having my fucking baby."

"Correction, we don't know whose baby this is."

"Stop being stupid. We already know that is my baby, so stop playing dumb. Julani, this whole time you haven't been doing anything but running from your true feelings. You are scared to let me in because you know that I am capable of breaking your heart worse than Messiah ever could. You're running from what you really want because you don't know how to handle the feelings that you have for me. You say you need time to focus on you, then let me help you with that. Let me help build you because I promise I will never tear you down. Allow me to be that nigga in your life who puts you in your place because you damn sure need it. I can help you become the woman you want and need to be. All you have to do is give me the green light ma and everything you ever wanted can be at your fingertips."

I talked all that shit about not fucking with her ass anymore and here I was, trying to make her mine. I just couldn't let her ass go. She was who I was destined to be with and she was who I was going to have, even if I had to kidnap that ass.

"I don't know what to say," she said, just above a whisper.

"You don't need to think of what to say, just say whatever is in your heart. It's as simple as that Julani."

We sat there in silence, looking at each other. My eyes were locked on her and hers were locked on mine. It was as if time slowed down. Whenever I stared into her eyes, I saw my future. That was the reason I was going so hard. Y'all could call me thirsty, a lame nigga, or even whipped, but it didn't matter because I knew what I wanted. I was man enough to go after who I wanted, especially when I saw the best in them. I saw the best in Julani, even when she didn't see it in herself.

"Cree, I want you," she whispered.

"Nah, I need you to tell me how you feel. You telling me you want me isn't good enough ma. We way past that point."

"Cree, when I say I want you, I'm not just talking about in a sexual way. I want you because my heart desires you. I've been trying to shake you since I met you, but I can't let you go. You are the last thing I think about before falling asleep, and you're on my mind when I wake up. I've known it was you, but I wanted Messiah, or at least I thought I wanted Messiah. After talking to my father, I honestly see that nothing good can come from Messiah and me. But with you, I see my present and future. With you is where I want to be."

I looked into her eyes to see if I saw any signs of uncertainty, but I didn't. Everything she was saying was what I've been waiting to hear her say.

"Ight. I need you to pack up your things and move into my crib with me this weekend. I don't want to hear shit about you're not ready or anything like that. You are pregnant with my child and I don't feel right with you living with your father. You don't need his support because you have mine."

"What do you mean I don't need his support?"

"You heard exactly what I said. I don't know your father all that well, but I do know that he is waiting for you to put some action behind all them words you be spitting. You talk a good game about you being a grown woman, but you still living with your father when you don't have to. Part of being a grown woman is paying bills and things of that nature."

"I do pay bills," she sassed.

"Paying your phone bill doesn't count Julani. I'm not saying that you have to pay bills in my house, because I got that covered. What I'm saying is that it's time for you to finally step out on your own baby. You need to spread them wings and fly. Of course, your father is going to be there to help you when you fall, but it will blow his mind to see you get up on your own, dust yourself off and take off."

Everything I was spitting to Julani right now was real shit. She wanted to work on herself and I was here to help. One thing I wasn't going to do is spoil her ass. Her father already did that, and now it was time to break her out of that habit. I was determined to help Julani become the woman she needed to be for our child.

"Okay, I hear what you're saying. I think you should come over and let my father know."

"I'll come with you to your crib, but you will be telling your father about the plans that we have. It's time for you to stand on your own two."

"Fine!" she said, pouting.

"Stop with all that pouting shit too. Now go in the kitchen, get an apple and let's go," I told her.

Before she could walk out the room, I walked towards her and pulled her into my arms. Her body melted into mine, as our child kicked.

"You felt that?" she asked, looking up at me with the biggest smile on her face.

"Yeah ma, a nigga felt that." I kissed her on the lips, then pulled her back into me.

A nigga was feeling good on the inside. Here I was, sitting with my nigga, listening to him talk about doing things big with Phallyn, wishing I could do the same, and now I was getting a chance to be able to go to the top with the woman that was made for me. A nigga was feeling real good at this moment. Wasn't nowhere but up to go from here.

Chapter 13: Messiah

"Amara, shut the fuck up with all that bitching. No one wants to hear that shit. You're pregnant, shouldn't this be a happy time?"

"How can anyone be happy when they are stuck with your miserable ass!" she yelled right back, poking me in my forehead.

I didn't know what to consider her since she thought I was miserable. This last week has been hell. Nah, fuck that, it has been worse than hell. Amara wouldn't stop talking about Julani, and as much as I loved hearing her name, I was tired of it coming from Amara's lip. The only thing that stopped me from wringing her fucking neck was the fact that she was pregnant. I promise you if there was no baby, I would put her ass out of her misery.

I was going through my own issues. Amara had me stuck in this fucking house with her ass. Whenever I would try to leave to get my fix, she would start up with the bullshit again. I was going through the withdrawal period and the shit was killing me. If I wasn't vomiting, then I would be sitting here crying or feeling agitated. I was going through it and all I needed was a quick line to make all the pain I was feeling go away. I just needed a line and then I would be able to deal with all of Amara's bullshit. I couldn't even think straight when it came to my plan with Julani because the cravings I had for that white lady overpowered my thought process.

"I'm so tired of your good for nothing ass Messiah. I should have let you stay with that bitch since that's where you want to be so bad. Go be with her and stress her the fuck out because I can't deal with this shit anymore. You know, I realized we fell out of love a long time ago, I just refused to let you go. I knew you had feelings for Julani way before you started to act on them. At first, I thought it was my eyes playing tricks on me, but after a while, I realized it. My heart just couldn't take the pain from losing you to some young bitch that barely knows how to blow her fucking nose. But right now, the way I'm feeling right now, she can have you because the hurt and pain you are causing me isn't even worth it anymore. Get the fuck out of my house, Messiah. I don't want you here!"

"Amara, shut the fuck up before you make me knock you out, ight. You act like you're the only one going through something. You don't see me yelling at you about not caring about me throwing up and shit. I'm dealing with shit just like you, so do us both a favor and go jump off of a fucking bridge or some shit."

"Nigga, what part of get the fuck out of my house don't you understand? You think I give a fuck about you going through withdrawals? Guess what nigga, I don't give a fuck about that shit. You brought that shit on yourself. You are a coward for turning to fucking drugs. You let a bitch get that far in your head that you turn to drugs to deal with her not wanting to be with you. Or was it the fact that the baby might not be yours that drove you to drugs? Huh, which one is it Messiah?"

"Amara, I'm telling you, get the fuck out my face with that shit. Go make a nigga a sandwich or some shit."

"Nigga, I'm not making your ass shit. You need to get the fuck out my house before I call the laws on your bitch ass. You have the nerve to get mad at me because I'm expressing how I feel. Your sorry ass is going to listen to everything I have to fucking say. You don't run shit over here no more Messiah."

"You're stressing my fucking baby out, move the fuck around Amara before I wring your fucking neck, damn. You get on my fucking nerves. You wanna talk about how I did you wrong and all this other bullshit. Don't nobody give a fuck about your feelings. Fuck your feelings, bitch. I wish I would've left your ass in the fucking group home where I found your raggedy ass. Matter fact, let's talk about that. The reason you have this fucking house to call your own is because of me. The reason that old ass dirty nigga isn't piping you down anymore is because of me. I bodied that nigga for you. Everything you got is because of this weak ass nigga over here.

You went out, day after day, spending my fucking money instead of earning your own. So you damn right I had feelings for Julani. You left the fucking door wide open for her to get her claws into me. Bitch, you weren't on your fucking job, so another bitch came and took over. Now you want to bitch and moan about the shit. Bitch you need to be sucking my dick and saying thank you for everything a nigga has done for you because without muthafucking Messiah, your ass wouldn't be shit. I made you ma. I upgraded you and put you into that new new. Bitch get over here and bless this mic, it's the least your loose pussy ass could do."

I moved the bucket I had been throwing up in to the side and pulled down my boxers, exposing my limp dick. I was dead ass serious about the shit too. She needed to thank me for all the shit I'd done for her.

"Really Messiah?" she said with tear stained cheeks. "You hate me that much you would bring up John's nasty ass. Especially after we made a pact not to say anything about it ever again. That's how the fuck you feel?" She inched closer to me as I held on to my dick, waiting for her to put her mouth on it. All that shit she was talking about was irrelevant to me right now.

"Fuck you, Messiah," she spat, picking up the bucket that had my vomit in it and throwing it at me. I was stuck for a minute because there was no way her ass just did that shit.

"Go suck your own fucking dick, bitch!" she spat. I went to lunge at her, but a knock on the door caught my attention.

"I'm fucking you up Amara, just wait and see." I walked over to the door, opening it without asking who was there.

"Nigga, you look like shit and you fucking stink. What the fuck is that on you?" King said, looking at me with disgust.

"If you would've hollered at a nigga and told him you were coming over, I would have cleaned up a bit," I smirked, walking away from the door.

"Messiah, you need help, and that's me keeping it one hundred," he told me, following behind.

I sat back on the couch with the throw up still on me, smirking. I didn't know what the fuck King wanted, but unless he wanted to get the same verbal lashing as Amara, I would suggest that he leave. Before all this shit, I looked up to King as a father. The same way I upgraded Amara, King upgraded me. The only difference was, I was now tired of walking in his shadows. His old ass needed to be on a beach somewhere, enjoying the fruits of his labor. Instead, he was still running shit. I was supposed to be the next king of the streets; it was only right since I would be dating his daughter. I smirked at the thought of me and Julani being the king and queen of the streets.

"Messiah, I know you fucking hear me talking to you. Respect me muthafucker before I put you out your misery." The fire in his eyes let me know he wasn't playing. For the time being, I was going to hear the nigga out, but when the time came for me to take over, I was laying his ass out. Julani would be mad, but as soon as I gave her this dick, she would be good.

"Wassup King? You were the last person I expected to see."

"Nigga, go put some fucking clothes on. I'm not talking to you with your fucking boxers on. Your dick is damn near hanging out. I'm not even on no homo shit either." I leaned over, grabbing the sweats that were next to me. I threw them on, then looked at him as if to say now what.

"Look, I need you to leave Julani alone, and this isn't a request either. You have way too much going on in your life right now. Julani is above all of this shit and I'm tired of you dragging her down with you. I already had this conversation with you when I first saw that you wanted to pursue my daughter. I let you know what it was, and you still played her ass. If you were any other nigga, you would be six feet under. But since I looked at you as a son, I will spare you your life."

I burst out laughing because King really thought he was that nigga. Well he was that nigga, but I wasn't like his other workers that feared him. I felt as though I was on the same level as him and he needed to treat me as such.

"As long as Julani is carrying my baby, I will forever be in her life. You letting me live, that's funny as fuck. I'm living because there is air in my lungs, not because someone allowed me too. King, you know how I get down."

"Messiah, you need to stay off them drugs because they fucking you up. Let me bring your scrawny ass up to speed real quick. All it takes is a snap of the fingers and poof, nigga you gone. You acting real brave like you want to challenge my gangsta. Remember I got the whole city of New York on my back. Like I fucking said, leave my daughter alone because nigga if you come within five feet of her, you're fucking gone, ight. I don't even give a fuck how you feel about the situation either."

"King, I'm not those corner boys you got shook. I'm a grown ass man and you need to treat me as such. Like the fuck I said, as long as Julani is pregnant with my child, I will always be around. She can talk that shit about it being that other nigga's, but I know the truth. She's carrying my baby Pop, so you might as well get used to me being around."

"You a real funny nigga, you know that Messiah. I honestly hope you get the help that you fucking need because them drugs are frying your brain. Since you're not listening to what I'm saying, let me put some fucking action behind it."

I watched him swiftly pull out his gun and in two seconds, I had a burning sensation coming from my foot.

"That was a warning shot. Test my gangster if you want to and the next one will be to the dome. Stay the fuck away from mine because I'll kill behind my fucking daughter, and I don't just mean you either," he smirked.

Looking past me, I turned my head and saw Amara peeking from around the kitchen corner. I wanted to tell her ass to get the fuck upstairs, but decided against it. I stared at King as he walked out of my house. The scream I was holding in while he was here, I finally let out. The nigga shot me in my fucking foot and that shit hurt like hell.

"Amara, come over here and help me into the bathroom. Then grab my phone so I can call someone up to clean this shit up," I barked.

"What makes you think I'm going to fucking help you? Especially after all that shit you talked to me."

"I swear on my unborn child if you don't bring your ass the fuck over here, I'm going to kill you with my fucking bare hands."

"Which unborn child are you talking about?" she laughed.

"Ight, Amara. My bad, ight. I'm sorry for the way I talked to you. I shouldn't have disrespected you or brought up John. You were talking to me greasy and I felt as though I needed to hurt your feelings the same way you were hurting mine. It's no excuse tho."

"Messiah, how do you expect me to believe that weak ass apology?"

"When have you ever known me to apologize?"

"True."

"These drugs are getting to me ma and fucking up my head. Yeah, I started doing drugs because I didn't know how to handle the shit Julani told me. That shit hurt me because I loved her. I honestly loved her and to find out she played me the way she did killed me. A part of me died on the inside. I didn't know how to survive, Amara. Then I started doing lines and history was made. I know this has to be hard for you to hear, but I feel like if we are going to have any chance at moving past this, I need to be straight one hundred with you. I loved Julani more than any other woman in this world. I thought Julani was supposed to be it for me. I thought she was the one, but just like I cheated on you, she cheated on me. So, I know how you feel and I understand everything you're going through right now. I know it's not easy to be pregnant by a man that is in love with another woman, but if you are willing to fix this, then so am I. I'm ready to put in work to get you back to the way you were. I destroyed the woman that you used to be. I will never be able to fully forgive myself for that. I'm here bleeding like a motherfucker from my foot, asking you to give me one more chance to make it right. One more chance to be the man that you need me to be. I'm here willing and ready to play by your rules, as long as I get you in return."

"Okay, Messiah," she whispered.

"Say that shit louder for a nigga."

"I said, okay Messiah. Now let's get you cleaned up so you can get your foot checked out before you bleed to death."

"That's my baby. Fuck Julani because I got my baby right here. I got me a winner."

Amara didn't respond to the last thing I said and that was okay. I got her right where I wanted her. If her ass thought I would pick her over Julani, her ass was sadly mistaken. I just need her on my side for the time being, but trust me, it wasn't going to be for long. As soon as I got shit together, I was deading her ass and coming for my baby, Juju. King could be the nigga for now, but I was coming for his ass. The same fear everyone had for him, was going to be the same fear niggas had for me. Payback was a fucking bitch and every nigga was catching bullet holes, especially that Cree nigga. Y'all thought it was bad when a chick was jealous, but y'all ain't never seen what happens when a nigga gets jealous.

Chapter 14: Amara

I know there are a couple of bitches out there that are calling me stupid, but that's only because they don't know my story. Y'all only know of Julani because she is the center of attention for everyone. I swear I couldn't stand that bitch and it wasn't because I was jealous of her ass or anything. I didn't like her off the simple fact that she could do no wrong. No matter what she did, everyone was always so forgiving and shit. She was basically Messiah's side chick and still came out of everything unscathed, while I looked like the stupid broad for constantly taking Messiah back.

I can admit I should have left Messiah when he first started fucking with Julani. If we really wanted to get technical, I should have stopped fucking with him once I knew he was no longer in love with me. Everyone thought Messiah and I were head over heels for each other, but that wasn't even the case. I loved him more than I loved myself. I loved him more than he loved me and that is where we went wrong. In a relationship, there shouldn't ever be a time when one person is more in love than the other. As soon as that happens, the relationship was doomed.

I realized Messiah wasn't in love with me four years into our relationship. I was the one sending him texts, saying that I missed him. I was the one telling him that I wanted to spend time together. I was the one putting in all the effort to make sure that we were okay. The only thing he cared about was getting his dick wet, and then getting back to work. Most times, I had to beat the words I love you out of him. Our relationship lacked love and compassion, but I was adamant about holding on because he was all I knew. Let's not forget he saved me from John.

Before Messiah came to the group home where I lived, our care taker John used to always sneak into my room. I cried silent tears as John had his way with me. He told me if I told anyone what was going on, I would end up a prostitute on the streets. I weighed my options and figured one dude sleeping with me was better than multiple men sleeping with me in a day. It went on for years, until Messiah came along. I instantly clicked with him and we became great friends. He was so different than the rest of the people in the group home and that intrigued me. Everywhere he went, I was right behind him. I looked up to him as a brother, but that all changed once our lips touched. Our lips connected and that's when I realized I wanted to be more than friends with Messiah. He tried to go all the way with me, but I started crying before he could enter me. He didn't know what was wrong with me, so he left me alone for a week. After the week, he came to me, asking me what had made me cry.

I tried my best to keep the secret, but Messiah seemed so loving and caring. I gave in, telling him everything. To say he was furious would be putting it nicely. The next night, he waited for John to come in my room like he usually did, and when John laid his body on top of mine, Messiah went behind and stabbed him in his back, then slit his throat. It was a good thing I had my own room because if I didn't, we would have been caught for sure. We snuck out after gathering our stuff, and that was the start of what would be our relationship. Till this day, I'm still surprised that we didn't get caught, but I counted my blessings that we didn't because I would never be able to survive being in jail.

Throughout our whole relationship, I allowed Messiah to run everything, including me. He didn't want me working because he was the man and he was supposed to be the one to provide. All he asked of me was to have dinner made when he got home and to have my legs open and ready, whenever he wanted it. I thought I was living the life, so I didn't really say much. The shopping sprees I went on that were once fun started to become boring. I was falling out of love with Messiah and I knew it. I should have walked away when Julani came into the picture because that was my escape, but for some reason, I felt disrespected. I felt like I had to fight for my man and let her know that we were strong. Because I fought for my man, I was now watching some nurse bitch clean up his wound from the corner of the bedroom.

I reached in the door next to me and pulled out the .22 Messiah had stashed there. I toyed with the idea of ending Messiah's life. Messiah to me wasn't worthy of breathing the same air as me. Everything he said to me earlier kept replaying in my head. How he confessed his love for Julani enraged me. There was no way I was going to bring a baby into all of this chaos. Messiah talked a good game, but whenever he mentioned Julani's name, there was a sparkle in his eye. It was as if his heart skipped a beat when her name was mentioned. He thought he was gaming me, but he wasn't.

He was right, it pained me to be pregnant by a man who was in love with another, but what hurt even more was the fact that he would still chase after her when a threat was made. King said in so many words that he would harm me and my unborn child if Messiah didn't stay away from Julani. There was no way in hell Messiah was going to stay away. Julani was his real drug of choice and he needed her to reach that high I couldn't bring him to. He needed her the same way a normal person needed oxygen. Julani was Messiah's reason to live, and I couldn't allow him to put me and my child in danger.

Speaking of my child, he barely acknowledged my child. The past week he has been back home, he never once asked how the baby was doing. I tried showing him sonogram pictures, but he wasn't for it. He would bitch and moan about not wanting to see that shit. My child didn't matter because Julani wasn't carrying her. The more I thought about everything, the clearer my decision became. Why should Messiah be able to live happily ever after when no one else was going to be able to?

"Okay, you should be fine. Just take it easy for the next couple of months," the nurse told Messiah.

"Ight, thanks ma. Amara, come walk her out for me." I placed the gun back in the drawer and walked the nurse out of the house. For a second, I stayed downstairs, working up the nerve to do the inevitable.

This has to be done. You are doing what's best for you and your child. I was giving myself a pep talk because I didn't think I was going to be able to go through with it. *He doesn't deserve to live Amara. You know this is the right thing to do. You have to eliminate your enemies so you can be happy. For once Amara, put your happiness first.*

I took the stairs, two at a time, ready to do what I never thought I would do. My hands were sweating and trembling as I opened the bedroom door we once shared. Now was the time to put an end to all of this.

"Amara, a nigga is hungry. Cook us something to eat and then we can sit and talk some more," Messiah called.

"Okay, anything for you," I called out, trying to steady my voice.

"I mean it, Amara. It's all about me, you and our baby."

"I'm glad that it's finally about us," I shouted back.

I assumed he was in the bathroom because I heard water running. Back in the day, Messiah taught me how to handle a gun, but I never had to put my skills to use. Shit, I didn't even know if I still had skills. Slipping on a pair of black gloves, I went and pulled the gun out. I didn't remember where the safety was so I quickly grabbed my phone off the bed and YouTube how to take the safety off. Once that was done with, I held it in my hand. I inched closer and closer into the bathroom, battling with myself. I wasn't sure if this was something I wanted to do, but how could I not go through with it. The gun was already in my hands, so there was no turning back.

I stepped into the bathroom, pulled the curtain back and pulled the trigger before Messiah could realize what was going on. One shot fired, then the next, and the next, until the clip was empty. I stood there, looking at Messiah's lifeless body drop into the tub. I didn't plan on filling him up with bullet holes, but once I started, I couldn't finish. A rush of adrenaline came over me. I instantly got hyped up and felt as though I was on top of the world.

I threw the gun in a duffle bag, packing up all my shit. I wasn't going to be connected to this in anyway. I went over the house twice, making sure I had everything. I moved all my bags to the front door, but ran down to the basement. Pulling out a baggy of coke I took off of Messiah when he first came back home, I ran back to the bathroom, where Messiah's lifeless bodied lied, and spread the coke against the sink. Hopefully, this will give the cops an idea that it was drug related.

It was dark out, so no one saw me leave out. I drove off with no real destination. With Messiah out of my life, I was free, or so I thought. It seemed as once I handled one problem, another one arose. My new problem went by the name of Julani Cortez. Getting close to her was going to be hard, but this was something that had to be done. If I could take out Messiah with little to no effort, then Julani wasn't going to be an issue. Once that was handled, I had plans on leaving the state of New York because there was no longer anything here for me.

Chapter 15 Julani

Two months later

Today was the day Cree and I were going to tell my father that I was moving in with him. For the past two months, I have been putting it off because I didn't know how I was going to tell my father. My father was all I had and I was all he had. I thought us living apart would be weird, so I put it off for so long. The excuses I was telling Cree before were no longer working. He wanted me all moved in before the baby came, which was in two more months. Not to mention, I still haven't started planning my baby shower. Right after the meeting with him, I needed to get up with Phallyn. I was seven months and couldn't wait to meet my son.

"Juju, bring your ass on, all you're doing is going to talk to your father."

"Don't rush me. It's kind of hard to move fast when you have a baby living in your stomach."

"Just bring your sexy ass on."

I blushed and followed him out the house. He helped me into his car, before pulling off. I stared out the window, thinking about how much everything has changed for me in the past two months. Allowing Cree into my heart was the best move I could've ever made. He made me feel loved and so at peace with everything in the world. He made me feel the way I wanted Messiah to make me feel. What I wanted in Messiah is what I ended up finding in Cree. It might have taken me some time to realize it, but I was happy I finally came to my senses.

I was about to tell Cree how much I appreciated him, when my phone started ringing. I looked at the caller ID and saw that it was my father.

"Hey daddy, I'm on my way to the house now, wassup?"

"Is Cree with you?"

"Uh, yeah he is. What's wrong?" My father wasn't talking like himself. It was like there was a shot of panic in his voice.

"Nothing is wrong, I'll see you when you get here," he said and hung up the phone. I looked at the phone in disbelief because my father has never just hung up on me like that.

"Wassup Juju, talk to me," Cree said, looking at me from the corner of his eye.

"Nothing, my father just called and ask me was I with you. When I tried to ask him what was wrong, he just said nothing and hung up the phone. My father never just hangs up the phone on me, something has to be wrong."

"I'm sure everything is okay. We're almost there, so we're gonna find out soon. Just relax and don't stress nothing until we find out what's going on, ight?"

I nodded my head yeah, but my ass was sitting here stressing the fuck out. As soon as my life was at peace, some bullshit wanted to come in to play. I didn't know what my father had to talk to us about, but I honestly didn't want to hear it. I was at a place in my life where I could smile just because. Messiah hasn't been a thought in the last two months, and neither has Amara. Something deep down was telling me that they were going to be the cause of my unhappiness.

* * * *

"Daddy!" I called out, walking in the house. Cree was holding my hand, squeezing it, trying to make me feel better. It wasn't really working, but I smiled at him so he wouldn't think I wasn't appreciative.

"Juju, stop all that damn yelling, I'm in the living room," he called out.

I led the way and found my father sitting with the TV off, and a cup of liquor sitting in front of him. "So wassup daddy, what did you want to talk about?"

"Have either of you been in contact with Messiah?"

"No. Why would either one of us be in contact with him? You already told me to leave him alone, so why would I go against your word?" I answered.

"You have gone against my word before Julani, but that's neither here nor there. Messiah was found dead this morning." His attention quickly turned to Cree when he said that. I wanted to gasp, but held it in because I didn't want Cree thinking I cared.

"King, no disrespect, but you looking at me trying to find any sign that I did it is a waste of time. It's no secret I wanted to body

Messiah, but that's not even me. I run with killers, so there is no need for me to get my hands dirty."

"I can respect that, but you know I had to ask. He wasn't killed this morning tho. Someone killed his ass about two months back, around the same time I told him to stay the fuck away from Juju."

"If he died two months ago, why is his body just now being found?"

"Someone randomly tipped off the police that there was a dead body in the house. Whoever killed him, just left his ass there. I wanted to get y'all over here to find out if either one of you had anything to do with it, just in case I need to clean up the mess."

"King, you don't even have to worry because if I did that shit, there would be no mess to clean. Not to mention, a nigga got a little dude on the way. I'm not trying to miss out on my child's life for some fuck nigga."

"That's that shit I like to hear," my father said, dapping Cree up.

The way they were talking and going about Messiah's death was weird to me. I didn't expect Cree to be effected because he didn't like Messiah to begin with, but my father was a different story. Messiah was like a son to him, and despite the bullshit he put me through, I still thought my father should care.

"How can you act like Messiah dying isn't a big deal? He was like son to you," I asked my father, cutting the side conversation him and Cree were having short.

"He was like a son to me, while you are my daughter. My daughter always comes first for me. The nigga that was like my son should have known how to treat my daughter. It's as simple as that. When I told him to stay the fuck away from you, he tried to boss up on me like I was just some regular nigga. That right there showed me he no longer respected me as a father figure. I can't pity a nigga who set himself up for his own downfall. Everything Messiah got is because of him. All he had to do was treat you right and everything would've been gucci. I know Amara's ass is somewhere happy as hell that the nigga is dead."

"Why would she be happy that her child's father is dead?" I was asking stupid ass questions, but none of this was making sense to me. Messiah was dead and everyone was acting as if it was a good thing.

"Just like Messiah was causing you pain and keeping you in a never ending loop, he was doing the same to her. The same pain you were feeling, was the same pain she had to deal with," Cree said.

I guess he was right, but the way she kept coming at me, you would think she was really head over heels in love with that nigga. Speaking of Amara, where the fuck was see when Messiah was being killed? I wasn't going to ask anyone that because it wasn't my business. My gut was telling me she was the one that killed Messiah, and you know what they say about a woman's gut.

"Juju, are you here to finally pack up your things?" my father asked, pulling me away from my thoughts.

"Huh, what are you talking bout?"

"You can cut the shit Julani. Tell your dad wassup," I glared at him while my father laughed.

"Chill on my baby girl," my father smiled.

"Let him know daddy," I giggled. "The real reason we came over here was to talk to you. As you know, I have been spending a lot of time with Cree and we both think it's best that I move in with him."

"Damn, so you're trying to leave me?"

"I'm not trying to leave you. I just think that it's time for me to be a grown up about things. You know my whole life I depended on you because you were always there and I think that was part of my problem. I need to learn to not depend solely on one person."

"I hear everything you're saying and I'm proud of you baby girl. Cree came to me a month ago and told me he wanted you to move in with him. I think Cree is good for you. As far as him being the man in your life, he has my blessing."

"Wait, you told him a month ago?" I asked, shocked. I didn't know my father and Cree had conversations with each other.

"Yeah, I told him. He's your father, so of course I wanted his blessing," Cree said, kissing me.

"Ight, enough of all that mushy shit. I'm taking both of y'all out to get something to eat," my father said.

We all got up and left out. Messiah's death was heavy on my mind because shit just wasn't adding up for me. There had to be more to the story, but what could I do at seven months pregnant. I decided to not let it bother me because Messiah was no longer my problem. I was focusing on the future, and he wasn't in it.

Chapter 16: Amara

I have been staying at a friend's house for the past two months, trying to come up with a plan on how to get at Julani. It would be my luck that her, her other baby daddy, and King would walk into IHOP, right before I did. If this wasn't a sign, then I didn't know what was. The stars have aligned and told me that this was my chance. I knew I was only going to get one, so I had to do this right. I got back in my car and waited for them to come out. I knew King and Cree weren't going to let me get close to Julani. I figured I would follow them until I caught Julani by herself.

Hours passed and I was still waiting in my car for someone to come out. It was a good thing I had two bags of chips in my car because a bitch would have starved waiting for them to come out. While eating my chips, my thoughts went to Messiah. I watched the news constantly, waiting to see something about his death. There were no reportings on his death and that made me nervous. It had been two months since I killed him and there was nothing. I called the anonymous tip line and told them there was a dead body in the house. I gave the operator the address and everything. I made sure to use a voice change over so then they wouldn't be able to use the audio to find me. Needless to say, there were news reportings this morning about Messiah's death.

Did I feel bad about killing him? No, I didn't because he deserved it, just like Julani deserved to die. My child was going to be brought into this world without a father, and it was going to be her fault. It was only right that she paid with her life for me and my child's pain and suffering.

"Thank you daddy for breakfast, or should I say brunch. I have to go meet up with Phallyn so we can plan this baby shower." It was crazy how close I was parked to them and didn't even know it. Just hearing her voice made me cringe. The jealousy I had for this girl was crazy. It's not that I wanted her life, I was jealous of the love Messiah had for her. The love he had for her was the love that I deserved. Her young minded ass didn't deserve anything, yet she got everything.

"Ight, you need me to drop you off?" Cree asked.

"I was hoping you would ride with my father and I could just take the car. I don't know how long I'm going to be out."

"Ight ma, that's cool. Make sure you call me when you meet up with Phallyn, and call me when you're leaving."

I watched as her father gave her a hug and a kiss, and then the other nigga did the same. I sat there looking on with envy. Julani got in her car first, while both guys stood and watched her drive off. When she drove past me, I ducked down, not wanting her to see me. When King and the other dude turned towards their car, I drove off, following Julani. I didn't have any plans on how I was going to kill Julani, but at this point, I didn't care. Everything was her fucking fault and she needed to pay. The only form of payment I was taking was her life.

I followed her all the way to an apartment complex. I pulled up right behind her and jumped out at the same time she did. I'm telling you, this was my lucky day because her ass parked in an alley, which was going to make killing her so much easier. For me to be eight months pregnant, I was moving pretty fast.

"Julani," I called out, with one hand behind my back. The gun I used to kill Messiah was going to be the same gun I used to kill her.

"Amara?" she asked, turning around with a raised eyebrow. "Amara, what are you doing here?" I could hear the panic in her voice and it was like music to my ears. For one, this bitch wasn't so comfortable, and there was no one to save her.

"Don't ask me questions bitch. You don't deserve to know what the fuck is going on."

"What are you talking about Amara? What you're saying doesn't even make sense."

"It doesn't have to make fucking sense!" I yelled. It angered me that she was right because what I was saying wasn't making sense.

"Look Amara, I'm sorry for your loss, but I have to go, okay?" She turned to walk away and that was when all hell broke loose.

"Bitch, don't fucking move!" I shouted, pulling out the gun.

She saw the gun and froze in place. A smile crept on my face as a look of terror appeared on hers. She placed both of her hands on her stomach, as if that was supposed to mean something to me.

"Amara, you don't have to do this," she pleaded.

"Shut the fuck up. Do you think I give a fuck about you trying to plead for your life? Did you give a fuck about me when you were sleeping with my boyfriend? Did you give a fuck about me then, huh?"

"I'm sorry, I was jealous that you had him. I thought I deserved him, but I was wrong. You deserved him so much more than I did. I know you have to be hurting behind losing him Amara. I understand that, but I can't help you unless you put the gun down. I will do everything in my power to make sure that you and your baby have everything that you need. I promise I will help you Amara."

"Me hurting behind Messiah's death, bitch you must be delusional. Messiah wasn't shit and he wasn't ever going to be shit. If you ask me, I gave that muthafucker exactly what he deserved."

"Wait, you killed Messiah?" The look she had on her face was priceless because she honestly just put two and two together. At that moment, she pulled out a gun that I didn't even know she had.

"Bitch, I'm going to tell you once to put the gun down before I kill you. Amara, I don't want to do this, so please don't make me. You are pregnant, the same way I am. We have kids to live for. Please don't do this."

"Oh, you think this is real?" I laughed. I lifted up my shirt that I had on and showed her the prosthetic belly. "Bish, what baby?" I giggled.

My laugh was cut short because a bullet ripped into my shoulder. The bitch done fucking shot me. She turned around to try and waddle away, but I was able to get a couple of shots off. The first one ripped through her leg, causing her to fall to the ground. The next one pierced her back. I used all the strength I could muster up to walk up on her. I emptied the rest of my clip into her body, the same way I did Messiah.

Now they could both be together in hell, where they belonged.

Epilogue: Julani

"Julani!" my father yelled, causing me to jump out of my bed. I felt around my bed and it was soaking wet.

"That was the craziest dream ever," I whispered to myself.

"Julani, are you up?" my father asked, coming into the room.

"Yeah, I am now," I said, staring at him blankly. I was trying to make sense of that dream I just had.

"You okay? Why are you covered in sweat?" my father asked with a look of concern.

"You wouldn't believe the dream I just had."

"That must have been a serious dream, because you look spooked."

"Daddy, I was pregnant and there were two guys that could have been the father. One of them being Messiah."

"The fuck you mean one of them could have been Messiah? You and Messiah have something going on?" Messiah and my father were like father and son. They were close, so for us to be messing around would be a big no no.

"No daddy, I'm not messing with him. I'm just trying to tell you what happened in my dream. Anyway, in the dream, I was jealous of Amara because she was with Messiah and I thought he was supposed to be with me. Messiah and I started messing around and he promised to leave Amara for me. When I found out that he wouldn't leave her, I started messing with Cree."

"Who the fuck is Cree?"

"Daddy, I don't know, he was some guy in my dream, just let me finish. Amara and I both ended up pregnant and that's when all the drama happened. Messiah ended up on drugs and Amara killed him. Then she ended up killing me when I was seven months pregnant." For some reason, I put my hands on my stomach and started crying. It was a dream, but it felt so real. The bullet holes that pierced my body, I felt. It was like I was having an outer body experience. Matter of fact, it was more so like an epiphany.

"Juju, don't cry baby, it was just a dream." My father pulled me to him and started wiping the tears from my eyes. I leaned on his shoulder, allowing the tears to fall freely.

My father probably thought I was crying because of how crazy the dream sounded, but that wasn't the case. I was crying because I had intentions of waking up today and telling Messiah how I felt. The jealous girl I was in the beginning of the dream was exactly who I was right now. I wanted Messiah for myself because I felt as though Amara didn't deserve him.

I was crying because in a weird way, I saw my future and how things would end up if I allowed my jealousy to consume me. Now that I saw where my jealousy was going to lead me, I was letting my jealousy go, because having a piece of Messiah wasn't worth all the drama it would've caused. And it damn sure wasn't worth me losing my life behind. That dream was a wakeup call and I was going to take heed to it. Amara could have Messiah because I wasn't with the shits.

Ephiany: An intuitive grasp of reality through something (as an event) usually simple and striking

The End!!

TURN THE PAGE FOR A SNEAK PEEK OF

GUNZ & LACI: BLACK ROSE MAFIA

Chapter 1: Lacianne 'Laci' Bentley

"Lacianne, I'm telling you this because I love you; you're wasting your pussy. There are men out here that are cutting their dicks off to get what you have in between your thighs and you're not even using it. You need to get out and live a little, before it's too late," my little sister Nazi complained. I loved her to death, but she got on my last nerve. You see, she was the free spirit out of us two. While my head was always stuck in a book, she was out living life to the fullest extent. Don't get me wrong, Nazi took school seriously; I was just more into academics than she was.

"Why do you always have to bring that up? I don't need a reminder, okay? Mom bugs me about it enough already! Another thing, don't worry about my vagina!" I snapped.

"Don't get mad at me because you signed a deal with the devil."

"Nazi, stop it. Our parents are not that bad okay. They made a way for us when we couldn't find a way for ourselves."

"So we have to hand over our love life in return? I'm sorry, but I'm just not doing it."

"Nazi, I have a lot of work to do. I'll call you back tomorrow."

"You can try to rush off the phone all you want. Just remember your twenty-fifth birthday is in a week."

"I know Nazi, damn," I spat and hung up the phone.

I leaned back in my office chair, trying not to let what Nazi said get to me. Nazi just didn't understand. You see, my name is Lacianne Bentley; I'm the adoptive daughter to Shirley and Dennis Bentley. Shirley and Dennis adopted me when I was five, and my sister Nazi when she was two. We were a package deal. You couldn't get one without the other. At first, I was a little taken aback by the Bentleys. I didn't understand why they would want to adopt two African American kids when they were Caucasian. I later learned that they didn't care about our skin color, they just wanted two children to love and pass their legacy on to. Growing up, Nazi and I attended the finest schools the city of Mount Vernon had to offer. They spoiled us rotten as long as we stayed at the top of our class. Education was very important to my parents, and I could see why. My father was the head lawyer at Bentley and Co., a company passed down from his father. My mother was a very successful plastic surgeon.

With our parents being successful, it was only right that they wanted the same for us. I followed my father's footsteps and became the youngest criminal defense attorney at Bentley and Co. Nazi was finishing up her dual bachelor's degree in psychology and sociology at Clark Atlanta University. Our parents were very proud of us, but there was one thing my mother would always bring up. Marriage. For some reason, my mother and father were big on settling down and getting married early in life. They claimed it was because when you marry early, you and your spouse are able to grow together and build together. Deep down, I always thought it was something more to the story, I just never spoke on the situation. Just thinking about marriage brings up the deal me and my mother made.

I was sitting in my room with books sprawled all over my bed, trying to get some extra studying in before it was time for me to go take my exam. I heard a faint knock on the door and sucked my teeth. Everyone in the house knew it was crunch time for me. I was in my last semester of getting my master's degree.

"Not now, I'm studying," I called out, hoping whoever was at my door would go away.

"I just want to talk to you for a second. I promise it won't be long," she said, sticking her head in the door.

"Fine," I sighed.

"I just wanted to talk to you about life. I see you are working hard on getting your degree and I admire that; however, you're not going to find a husband while in them books."

"Mom, I don't have time to go out and find a husband right now. I'm twenty-three and about to have my master's, after I will be taking the bar exam. There is no room in my life to date right now." I barely had time to have sex. I only had sex about five times in my life, and that was usually when I went to visit my sister in Atlanta. She was dating some dude from her college who had an older brother. He was cute and understood the no strings attached logic, which made everything easier for me. I stopped messing with him a couple of months back, leaving me to be sexless.

"That's why I'm coming to you with a proposal," she beamed.

"What kind of proposal?"

"How about you let me and your father pick your husband for you."

"Like an arranged marriage?" I held in my laughter because I didn't want to offend her.

"If that's how you want to look at it."

"Fine ma, if I'm not in a serious relationship by the time I am twenty-five, I will allow you and dad to pick my husband."

"Okay, twenty-five it is. Happy studying baby," she kissed me on the cheek, then got up and left.

I didn't think she was serious about the situation, but as the years started to go pass, she would always bring up the situation. She went as far as bringing my dad's best friend's son around on my birthdays. If I would've known how serious she was, I would've never agreed to it.

"Sir, you can't go in there!" I heard my secretary say from outside my office.

"Sweetie, I go wherever I please," was the next thing I heard before my office doors busted open.

I sat up in my chair, taking in his appearance. If I had to take an educated guess, I would say he was about 6'4. He was dressed to the tee in a tailored made black Armani suit, with the all black Armani loafers. His hair was cut short, but it was long enough to see his soft curls. Dude was rocking the Rick Ross beard, but it was shorter and neater. His overall appearance and look was a nine, but what made him a ten were his eyes. They were as black as coal and for some strange reason, they were alluring to me.

"I'm so sorry, Lacianne. I tried to tell him that he couldn't just walk in here. Do you need me to call security?" Before I could speak up, the man standing in my office began to talk.

"No, she does not need security. What she needs is for you to leave out her office, close her door and go back to your desk and get some work done, instead of playing subway surfers."

My secretary looked at me and I just nodded my head, letting her know I agreed with what he said. I waited until my office door was closed to find out what he was doing in my office.

"Now, I don't know you and you don't know me, with that being said, I need for you to leave my office and talk to my secretary about making an appointment to see me."

"I don't do appointments sweetheart," he smirked, sitting in the chair that was across from my desk.

"Then I'm not the lawyer you need."

"The way I see it, we can help each other. You're a new lawyer here and word around the office is you're only here because of your pops. From where I sit, you have a point to prove, and I can help you prove that point."

"Just how are you going to help me 'prove' this point?" I was intrigued by this man, but at the same time, annoyed.

"I want to keep you on retainer."

"Yeah, you definitely do not need me as a lawyer because I don't do retainer. Unless you want me to call security so they can escort you out of here, I suggest you leave."

"What's your name again sweetheart?" he asked, with a lick of his lips.

"You know I'm new here and that I have a point to prove, but you do not know my name. In case you missed it on the front of my desk, my name is Lacianne," I sassed.

"Look here Laci, I don't care what you think you don't do, all I care about is what you're going to do. And what you're going to do is take this forty grand I have in this briefcase, along with my phone number." He lifted a briefcase I didn't even realize he had on my desk, opening it so I could see the money. He then took one of my business cards off my desk, scribbled what I presumed to be his number, flicked it at me, then got up, heading towards the door.

"Wait," I called out, still in shock at the way he just handled me. I never had a man talk to me the way he did.

"What you want Laci?" he asked, turning around.

"My name is not Laci, it is Lacianne," I corrected him. The only person that called me Laci was Nazi.

"Your name is whatever I want it to be. I hate repeating myself, but for you, I will make an exception. What do you want Laci?"

"What is your name?"

"Bryce Carter, but you can call me Gunz." With that, he walked out my office.

I swiped my hand over the money in the briefcase, sitting there in awe. I snapped it close and sat it under my desk. I looked at the card with his number on it, contemplating my next move. I stuck the card in the shredder, then called my secretary back in my office.

"Yes, Lacianne."

"Take this briefcase, box it up and have it sent out to a Mr. Bryce Carter. Please and thank you. Another thing, if any other potential clients catch you playing subway surfers, you will be out of a job." I handed the briefcase to my secretary and watched as she left my office. Bryce was very arrogant, cocky and entitled. As much as I did need to prove my worth at this company, I wasn't going to do it by helping Mr. Gunz.

Chapter 2: Bryce 'Gunz' Carter

"Yo, make sure you and Jinx is at the crib. I'll be there in thirty," I said to Jiselle, then hung up the phone. I placed my iPhone five back in my pocket, jumping into my 2014 Lexus is350. I cruised the streets of Manhattan, headed to my brownstone in Queens. I know from the way I talked to lawyer girl y'all probably thinking I'm some cocky asshole. I couldn't even deny it because it was the truth. A nigga was cocky as fuck, but I had every right to be. At the age of twenty-seven, I was out here getting it. I had a gang of young bulls ready to kill at a drop of a dime. Let me clear the air right quick, no I'm not a drug lord or the plug, that's the shit my pops was into. Even though my pops taught me the game, I chose to make my on lane. What nigga you know wanted to follow in another nigga's footsteps? Pops or not, I was determined to create something that was my own. It was hard to explain my profession because I was into a little bit of everything. I guess you could call me the secret service of the hood. I had techs on my team that could make the dirtiest record clean in a matter of minutes. I had snipers on my team that could kill a person from thirty feet away. A nigga was even fucking with a couple of assassins. Most importantly, I protected my parent's drug empire. What y'all might call illegal activity, I call Black Rose Mafia.

I didn't have the traditional relationship with my parents like most kids growing up. Our family was more about money, power, and respect, than it was about love. My pops, Stephan Carter, and my mother, Rose Carter, made sure that each of their kids had one skill that they were good at. My pops use to always tell us one may not always know his purpose until his only option is to monopolize in what he truly excels at. When I was younger, I didn't understand the shit my moms and pops were trying to teach us. As I got older and realized exactly what my skill was, I understood what they were trying to instill in us. You see, my skill is guns. I can handle just about any gun out there. I'm the deadliest sniper in Black Rose Mafia. Jinx's skill is technology. He is the best hacker of our generation. This nigga can hack into just about anything, which makes him just as deadly as me. Jiselle's skill is knives. My sister was a bad bitch in every sense of the word. She can slit a person's throat faster than someone can blink.

Our parents weren't the normal parents. They had that cliché Bonnie and Clyde relationship. What made them different was how they raised us. We didn't attend public school or private school. My parents felt there wasn't shit a school system could teach us that they couldn't. Jinx, Jiselle, and I were all home schooled. We did the work that was expected of us, but my parents always gave us extra tasks that would heighten our skill. Since skill was an important factor in our lives, I decided at the age of eighteen to capitalize off it. I started off killing for my father. Whoever he needed dead, I would handle that for him and he would pay me accordingly. Once my brother and sister saw I was making money, they wanted in. With Jinx's hacker skills, Jiselle and I became assassins; killing people for the cartels, the mob, and everything in between.

We were young and getting it, but at some point it became too much. We started recruiting young people from the hood that were looking for a come up. Instead of trying to figure out what their skill was, we taught them our skills. However, we never taught them too much to where they could turn around and use the skill against us. As our empire grew, we decided that we needed a name. Since our pops' crew was called Black Mafia, and our mother's name was Rose, we chose to combine the two, hence Black Rose Mafia. That was nine years ago and we were now seventy-five members deep. Black Rose Mafia was an empire, and I ruled it with an iron fist. Everyone in the hood knew of me and my siblings, but no one really knew us. Shit, to be in our presence was a blessing in itself.

I pulled up to my brownstone and hopped out my car. I jogged over to my mailbox, then rushed into the house to get away from the cool crisp air. It was the first week of February and winter wasn't playing with our asses. The snow didn't hit yet, but it was cold as shit outside.

I went into the kitchen to grab a bottle of water, then went to the living room, where I had an intercom installed.

"Yo!" I said, pressing the button. My brownstone was like a three family home. Jiselle lived on the top floor, I lived on the middle floor, and Jinx had the bottom floor.

"I'm coming down now," Jiselle replied.

"I'm coming up," Jinx said.

I sat on the couch, flicking on the TV, waiting for my siblings. Jinx was a year younger than me, and Jiselle was a year younger than Jinx. It was crazy how close the three of us were. I guess you could say since our parents didn't show us much love, we loved each other hard. My parents were still alive, I just didn't fuck with them unless business was involved, or it was Sunday dinner.

"How things go with the lawyer chick?" Jinx asked, walking in the living room, followed by Jiselle.

"Shit went ight. She tried to tell me she didn't do retainer, but you know I shut that shit down real quick. I told her ass what she was going to do and left her office like I owned the place," I chuckled.

"Bryce, what did I tell you about going into places, demanding shit? The sun does not rise and shine on your ass," Jiselle complained.

"You know you can't tell this nigga nothing," Jinx laughed.

"I could have sworn I was the nigga in charge. Am I not the nigga that started all of this?" I looked at my younger siblings, waiting for one of them to challenge my authority. I loved my brother and sister to death, but I didn't tolerate disrespect from anyone.

"Bryce, chill with all that I'm the king shit. We are your family, not your fans or entourage," Jiselle sassed.

"Nah, you need to chill out trying to tell me how to operate. If I wanted to walk in shawty's office demanding shit, then that is exactly what I'm going to do."

"All I'm saying is you could have gone about things in a different way. I don't even know why you want ole girl on our team anyway. I'm sure there are better lawyers than her." Jiselle rolled her eyes at me and poked her lips out. Jinx and I didn't really date much, which made Jiselle the sole female in our lives.

"I want her because she's hungry. She has a point to prove and is willing to go to war to prove it. I just need her to go to war for me if it ever came down to it."

"Yeah whatever, she just better stay out of my way."

"Why you acting jealous over a chick you don't even know yet?" Jinx asked.

"I'm not acting jealous, so shut up dummy."

"Jiselle, you don't have to worry, baby girl. No one is going to come in and take your spot. You know you're the number one girl in our eyes," I smiled.

"And that's how it better stay," she giggled.

"You sound like you want us to be gay or some shit?" Jinx said.

"Don't nobody want you to be gay. I just feel like no smut, thot, or whore should be put above me." She shrugged as if what she said was something we should've already known.

"What if we find a woman, then what? Are you still supposed to come first?"

"Jinx, if you ever find a woman in this generation, I will name my first born after you. I have a better chance finding a real ass nigga, then you do a woman. Shit, things have changed; men aren't really the hoes anymore, chicks are. I'm the last real woman on the planet," Jiselle laughed.

I couldn't help but to laugh with her because she was always saying some slick shit.

"Just remember that shit you said ight. I'm out of here though. I got some shit to handle," Jinx said, getting up.

"I guess it's just me and you tonight," I told Jiselle.

"Yup, so get dressed because we are going out to eat."

"You can just cook here. I don't really feel like going out. A nigga is tired," I yawned.

"I don't feel like cooking and you can't cook, so that means we are going out. I'll let you take a little nap, but just know I'll be up here at six, waking your ass up."

"Correction, I can cook and my shit always comes out better than yours. Don't try to play me sis. Now get out my house yo," I told her.

"I'm going to let you keep thinking that because it makes you feel better." She got up, hitting me with the peace sign and heading out the door. I stretched out on the couch, ready to catch some z's. Right before I drifted to sleep, the conversation I had with Laci replayed in my head. I kind of felt bad about the way I handled her. I made a mental note to send her some flowers as an apology. We were going to be doing business together and I didn't want to start off on the wrong foot.

* * * *

I yawned and stretched my lean body as I stepped out of my car. I traded in my suit for a pair of black G-Star jeans, beef and broccoli Timbs, an olive green hoodie and my black Moncler coat. Jiselle stood by my side, wearing the same exact thing. If you didn't know we were siblings, you would've thought we were doing the cute couple thing.

"Out of all places we could have went to eat, you wanted to come here?" Jiselle spat.

"Where did you think we were going? You wanted to go out to eat, so I'm feeding you. Don't act like you're too good for Buffalo Wild Wings."

"I'm not saying I'm too good, I just didn't think we would end up at a sports bar," she said and walked towards the entrance. I shook my head because Jiselle was too high maintenance and spoiled for me. Whatever dude locked her crazy ass down would be in for the ride of his life.

I was about to catch up with her, when something to my left piqued my interest. Getting out of her car was Ms. Laci. I watched her strut towards the entrance and I began walking in the same direction. Being the one with the longer stride, I made it to the door first.

"After you," I smiled, holding the door for her.

"If it isn't Mr. Bryce," she snickered, walking in the door. Her whole demeanor was off and I didn't like it. Before she could get to the greeter, I called out to her.

"Laci!" She looked back at me, rolled her eyes and continued the short distance to the greeter.

I walked right up on her as she was telling the greeter she just wanted to get take out.

I coolly grabbed her hand, pulling her back towards the entrance. I made sure to take long strides so her ass would wave to run a little to keep up. I brought her to my car and pushed her ass up against it.

"Did you or did you not hear me calling you?" I had my hands on both sides of her head, leaning on the car. She looked at me with so much confusion in her eyes.

"I uh…" she stuttered.

"It's a yes or no Laci."

"Yes."

"Then why did you ignore me? When I call out to you, you answer, ight? I don't play childish games, and neither will you. We are both adults, so you need to behave as such."

I didn't notice it before, but I damn sure was noticing it now. Laci was breathtaking and I'm not even talking about her body. She had the richest chocolate skin complexion I had ever seen. The glasses she wore did nothing but bring out her chestnut colored eyes that were slightly slanted. From her button nose to her plump pouty lips, Laci was perfect. From the looks of it, she didn't have on any makeup, and she didn't need any. Her natural beauty was more than enough. I unintentionally touched one of her curls, wrapping it around my finger. I let it go, then took a step back to get a better look at her. She was short as hell, from what I could see; she stood about 5'4. She was rocking a navy blue pants suit that was a little loose fitting, leaving me to imagine what her body looked like underneath all those clothes.

"Uh Bryce, I'm kind of hungry. If you don't mind, I would appreciate it if you would stop undressing me with your eyes and allow me to go place my order. I have a lot of work I need to get done tonight." I heard the nervousness all in her voice as she tried to be polite. I grabbed her hand once again and walked with her into the restaurant. I spotted my sister off in the distance, flirting with some dude. I led Laci to the take out line and stood with her.

"Why are you holding my hand?" Laci questioned.

"Why does it matter?" I asked right back.

"You are making it seem as if we are couple, and we aren't," Laci said in a hushed tone.

"If you think I'm making us look like a couple, then that is because you want us to be." I gently yanked her, moving her closer to me. I leaned down, bringing my face only inches away from hers.

"Laci, all those sexual thoughts you're having about me right now, you need to dead them. I will fuck your life up. I would have you thinking about taking a charge for me, and that's not even you. As far as I'm concerned, this is just business between the two of us. You are my lawyer and I'm your client. Do you hear me Laci?"

"Yes, I hear you."

"Ight then. Order your food, then call me when you get home so I know you're safe." I gave her a light kiss, then walked away, heading towards the table where my sister was waiting.

"What was all of that about?" she asked as soon as I sat down.

"That was nothing."

"Whatever big head."

I mushed Jiselle before looking over my menu. Laci didn't know it, but she was officially on my radar. I could tell from the way she allowed me to handle her that she was green to a lot of things. It was cool though because that meant I could mold her into the woman I wanted her to be. Ms. Laci was definitely someone I would begin to invest my time in. All dudes say they get what they want, so I'm not even going to use that line. I'll just leave it at, Ms. Laci will be Mrs. Carter in due time.

Chapter 3: Laci

Two days passed by and I haven't heard anything from Bryce. Since he was so adamant about me being his lawyer, I presumed he would be marching into my office the next day, demanding that I keep the cash I sent back to him. That obviously wasn't the case. He never showed up at my office or called. I felt a little hurt by the situation. I wasn't sure why, but Bryce consumed my thoughts so often. After the sweet, gentle kiss he gave me, I ran out of the restaurant, not even bothering to order my food.

The way he talked to me and handled me was intriguing. His approach wasn't like most dudes. Yes, he was rude and cocky, but it didn't make me want to slap him. The way he talked to me had me ready to call him daddy and ask what he wanted for breakfast. However, that was just silly thinking because the two of us would never work. I could tell from his demeanor we came from two different worlds. Let's not mention he needed a criminal lawyer on his team. There was no way in the world I was going to date a criminal. My little fantasies would just have to do, because Gunz was off limits.

The work day came and went pretty fast, and I couldn't be happier. My days started to blend together and I began to feel as if I was losing my mind. Being a criminal defense attorney was a lot of work. It wasn't anything I couldn't handle, I just had to get use to the process. I gathered all of my case files that needed reviewing over the weekend and headed down to my car. I threw my briefcase, along with the rest of my things on the backseat, and jumped in my car. I sat there for a second, trying to get my car to warm up. Even though I was a winter baby, I couldn't stand the cold. Spring and fall were more so my seasons. I drove home in silence as I did after every work day. The silence always helped my mind to unwind. I lived alone, but as soon as I stepped foot in the house, it was right back to work. My whole life consisted of nothing but work. I couldn't complain because work was the reason I was able to afford a beautiful two family home in New Springville located in Staten Island. I loved my house. I upgraded the whole house after a year of owning it. Hardwood floors, pella windows, granite countertops and stainless steel appliances decorated my home. The house had four bedrooms and three bathrooms, which was more than I needed. Nazi had her own room since when she came up from college, she would stay with me, instead of our parents. The other two rooms were supposed to be guest rooms, but they were really for show because I didn't allow anyone besides my family in my home. My home was my sanctuary, and I liked to keep it that way.

I parked my car in the driveway and headed for my front door. The case files I had in my backseat would have to stay there because this Friday night was going to be spent unwinding and soaking in a hot bubble bath. Walking inside, I kicked my shoes off at the front door and went straight for the kitchen. I pulled out a glass and a bottle of wine, ready to get my calm evening started.

As I poured my glass, I noticed a huge bouquet of ocean breeze orchids. Now upon seeing them, a couple of thoughts ran across my mind. The first was how did they get into my house and who were they from. I was grateful for them because they honestly were my favorite flower. The fact that they were in a cute purple vase with my name engraved made it all the more special. I walked over to them, guessing my mother or father sent them as an early birthday gift.

I smelled the flowers, loving the scent, before looking for a card. I grabbed the card from in the middle of the bouquet.

Laci,

I see that you're a difficult one, but a challenge isn't something that I back down from. Orchids symbolize perfection & beauty. So imagine my surprise when your favorite flower is the ocean breeze orchid. I already knew you were beautiful and perfect, but now I can add rare to that list. The money that you sent back to me is in your bank account. Don't question how, just simply smile and enjoy your flowers.

Gunz

An unexpected smile spread across my face. I grabbed my phone off the counter and quickly went to my Citibank app. I hurriedly signed in and lo and behold, my bank account had an extra forty grand. I moved the flowers from the counter and sat them in the middle of my island. I shook my head as I picked up my glass of wine and headed for the staircase. I climbed the stairs, ready to soak in my tub, when I heard music coming from Nazi's room. I rolled my eyes and went towards her door. Not really caring about respecting her privacy, I opened the door to find her dancing around her room to a Beyoncé song.

"Nazi, what are you doing here? You're not supposed to be here until next weekend. My birthday is the 14th, remember?" I asked, turning down her music.

"I'm your sister, how could I forget your birthday? Not to mention, your birthday is Valentine's Day."

"Yeah, well you could have given me a heads up that you were coming."

"You could have given me a heads up that you were dating someone," she smiled, pulling me over to her bed.

"What are you talking about? I'm not dating anyone."

"You don't have to lie, Laci. He sent you your favorite flowers and those are not easy to get. As soon as I got here, the doorbell was ringing. The delivery guy didn't even want to give them to me because he had strict instructions to give them to you. He even had a picture of what you look like. Is the dude you're dating in the FBI? If so, tell him I have a couple of tickets he can get rid of," she laughed, but I didn't find anything funny.

I was thankful, but creeped out at the same time. I couldn't figure out how he knew my favorite flower, where I lived and he had a picture of me to give to the delivery guy. Not to mention, he put money in my back account. I hope he wasn't a stalker or anything because I would hate to have to move.

"So who is he?" Nazi asked, taking me out of my little rant I was having in my mind.

"He's not my boyfriend, he's my client that just might be a stalker."

"A stalker! Did you tell dad? Matter of fact, he wouldn't know how to handle a dude that goes by the name Gunz. I'll give you the lipstick stun gun I have. You need it way more than I do."

"Where the hell did you get a stun gun from? You do know it's illegal, right?"

"Sissy, it's only illegal if you get caught. Any who, let's go out tonight."

"I don't want to. Why don't you go up the street and go visit mom and dad?" I lived a couple of blocks away from my parents. They were part of the reason I was able to afford this house. I paid for the house with most of my money, but their names were the ones on the dotted line.

"They don't even know I'm up here and I would like to keep it that way. Come on Laci, come out with me. I want to go to a reggae club," she smiled.

"You think you are so slick." I gave her the side eye because she knew I loved me some reggae. Mavado was my weakness, I repped the gully hard.

"Fine, if you're not having fun, then we can leave."

"Okay Nazi, I'll go," I sighed, sipping on my wine.

"Good and I'll pick out your outfit, so don't worry. Go get in the tub so you can soak because I know that's what you were going to do. I'll have your clothes out on the bed."

"Don't try to dress me in anything too revealing, Nazi."

"I won't, relax. Now get out my room so I can finish listening to my music."

I rolled my eyes at her and left out the room. I went straight for my master bathroom and turned on the hot water in my free standing tub. I added a couple of drops of vanilla oil and some vanilla scented bath salts. I sat my cup of wine at the edge of the tub, before going into my room. I stripped out of my clothes, leaving them on my bedroom floor. I turned on my heels to go back in my bathroom when my house phone started ringing.

"Hello?" I answered, walking towards my bathroom. I lowered myself into the steamy bath water, trying to get comfortable.

"Did you like the flowers?" his deep voice said through the phone. His voice was raspy, but sensual at the same time.

"Yes, I did like my flowers, but I'm starting to believe you're a stalker. First, you get my address to send me flowers, then you somehow get my bank account number to send me money, and now you have my home phone number." I had to stay calm because I didn't know if he was a lunatic or not. For all I know, he could be sitting outside my house.

"Baby, there is no need for me to be a stalker because a nigga like me got a flock of bitches ready and willing to do anything I need them to."

"Oh really?" I said, feeling a twinge of jealousy. "Why don't you go keep one of your bitches company and get off my phone." Something about him saying he had other women bothered me.

"Calm down, Laci. No need to be jealous because we aren't even together. Like I said, this is all business between us."

"Okay."

"I just wanted to call you and make sure you liked your flowers." I could hear a laugh in his voice.

"Then you could have called my office phone and left a message."

"I don't do messages, plus calling your house phone is more intimate. I can bet the only people who have your house number are immediate family."

"You are absolutely right. Calling my house phone is more intimate, and intimate we are not. Anything else you need concerning business, you can reach me at my office," I hung up the phone feeling pissed off.

Bryce was so confusing. I may not have been into dating, but I knew when someone was flirting with me. He would flirt with me, then throw it in my face that we only had business together. I didn't even want to have business with him, but I didn't have much of a choice since he put it in my bank account. I was going to keep him at arm's length because I still felt he was borderline crazy.

LAF
NOU

Made in the USA
Charleston, SC
25 November 2016